Eyes of Gray

Dani O'Connor

2007

Spinsters Ink
P.O. Box 242
Midway, Florida 32343

Printed in the United States of America on acid-free paper
First Edition

Editor: Anna Chinappi
Cover designer: Stephanie Solomon-Lopez

ISBN10: 1-883523-82-6
ISBN 13: 978-1-883523-82-4

This book is dedicated to my college roommates Susan, Beth and Kirsty.
I miss those days on the porch. Above all . . . I miss you.

Acknowledgments

Thank you to my family: John, Patty, Brooke, Dad, Diana and Erik.

A very special thank you to my mom who always points me in the right direction.

Thanks to Linda at Spinsters Ink for indulging me a second time.

Thank you, Anna, my editor, for all of it. Once again, you made it all better.

About the Author

Dani O'Connor is the biggest dreamer in all the suburbs.

Chapter 1

I awoke to the sound of church bells. The deafening, clinging clamor was enough to beckon the believers and provoke the sinners. The fact that I was still in bed confirmed my membership in the latter category and not the Latter-day Saints. I lay in bed with pillows pushed against my ears and regretted renting the house across the street from the oversized Methodist church. The bells continued for what seemed like an eternity and I forced myself back to sleep.

Round two. Again with the bells, the incessant hollering that rang through my head like an alarm clock with no volume control. I pulled myself from under my warm covers and dragged my tired body to the kitchen. I managed to scrape together enough instant coffee and stale milk to fill one large plastic Circle K mug. I dropped the last twelve kibbles of cat food into the plastic fish-shaped bowl and pretended it was a meal fit for a king. I made my escape to the other room before my three cats had a moment to complain.

The clock read 8:40. When adjusted for the actual non-daylight savings time, I knew it was really 9:33. I turned on the TV forgetting that the cable had been shut off weeks earlier due to lack of interest in paying the bill. I hoped that my check went through to the local paper so that I would at least have my Sunday news. I was in luck, the rolled up bulk of pages rested safely on my doorstep—one more check had eked its way through the system. I flipped and re-flipped my way through the sections until I located the Daily Life which contained my mandatory weekly routine—the Sunday crossword.

The weather report on page two called for partly sunny skies and temperatures in the seventies. I never understood the difference between partly sunny and partly cloudy. I figured it was something like the difference between depression and mild depression. Either way, I was delighted that the rain would hold off until Monday. I decided to take my paper and coffee to the front porch so I could get the full effect of the unusually warm April morning. I buried myself in the crossword and didn't notice the cars and voices around me.

The church bells chimed one last time, a way of saying "last call" to the people lingering outside. I glanced up to see a trailing group of parishioners hurry through the bulky wooden doors. I never paid serious attention to the Sunday morning group, normally I hid myself inside until the noon "all clear" bells. Today, I took the time to watch the crowd and was pleasantly surprised. I was completely off with my assumption that they were all a bunch of old ladies in polyester pantsuits and kids in starched cotton jumpers. I saw a variety of churchgoers I never expected—bouncy teenage girls full of smiles, middle aged, plaid-suited men leering at the single mothers, even college-age men looking hung over and slightly irritated. I watched them all enter the doors of the beautiful, stoic building as I drank my lukewarm coffee and reminisced of my own Sunday school days. I remained on my squeaky porch swing for the rest of the morning. I watched the comings and goings of people during all the services. I was surprised to see some of the same people attending more than one sermon. I referred to them as the "second comings." I observed their behavior, I eavesdropped on their gossip, I admired their clothes and I even wrote down the names of the people I recognized.

One stranger bewildered me. He stood outside the church and watched my street. He never went inside, he paced from the church door to the curb to the pay phone on the corner. He chain-smoked and lit each cigarette with a Zippo, not one cigarette off the other like most chain-smokers do. He never looked my way and I never saw his face. I found it odd that he was wearing a black trench coat on a beautiful spring morning. A faded black fedora hid his eyes. His subtle limp almost seemed contrived. He took the same number of steps on every pacing route. He never talked to anyone and he never looked my way. The eerie thing was his familiarity. I knew this man—I'd subconsciously known him for years although I never acknowledged his existence. A chill went up my spine and I retreated to the safety of my sparsely furnished college rental.

I was pretty much stuck with the house. I initially had three roommates who, through their brilliance or lack thereof, had managed to either graduate early or get kicked out of the university. We had signed a three-year lease and I was obligated to the place for nine more months. I was to graduate in the fall, There was no need to break the lease. The thought of taking on some new roommates crossed my mind occasionally but I didn't feel like putting up with other people's issues during my senior year. I decided it was better to just get a job to make up the difference in rent. I started working four nights a week at a local bar and grill. It cut into my study time and social life but it was worth it to have a nice house near campus.

The house was built in 1919 and had the creaky wooden floors to prove it. It was a two-bedroom plan with a sunporch and studio connected to the back. We managed to make it a four-bedroom house by converting the studio and the large dining room into bedrooms. When we moved in, I staked my claim on the small studio area because I liked the view of the backyard and I liked having a door that led directly to the sunporch. It was about half the size of the other rooms but I didn't care. I shoved my bed in the corner and kept most of my clothes in boxes. Even after the other girls moved out, I continued sleeping in the studio and left the other rooms empty.

The best part of the house was its location. It was nestled on the corner with the church across the street and the university's language building on the diagonal. Every year, the homecoming parade would march right past our front door. We were able to walk to every building on campus and every seedy college bar in town. We became known as the party house and every weekend after the bars closed, friends and strangers would find their way to our happy home. My favorite part of the house was the huge front porch. We added a precarious wooden swing and a few benches. The four of us spent hours on that porch studying, drinking, gossiping and loving our youth.

On the corner next to the church was a pay phone. One year during a street fair, we walked over and got the number. We spent the rest of the weekend sitting on the porch and calling the phone as strangers walked by. We were always amazed at the number of people who would answer a public phone. Most of the time we would tell them they left their lights on. Sometimes we told them their fly was open. Occasionally we would see a cute guy walking past and we'd call the phone and invite him to join us on the porch. One of my roommates met her husband using that gag.

I felt a huge attachment toward the house because it held the greatest memories of my life. I was a little nervous about the man in black spending the day across the street but I decided not to give it a second thought. I certainly wasn't going to abandon my wonderful house because of a little insecurity.

Chapter 2

I woke up late Monday morning. My first class was at eight and my cheap alarm clock went off an hour past its setting at 7:40. This was one of the times I appreciated my proximity to campus. I didn't have to mess with parking, I merely had to walk a block and a half to my logic class in Canon Hall. I bolted out of bed, threw on dirty jeans from the top of the pile, grabbed a Diet Coke from the fridge and pretended not to see my cats as they chased me down the hall to the front door.

I was halfway down the block when I felt a cold chill run down my spine. Something possessed me to stop my slow jog and turn around. My stomach sank as I glanced around and saw the dark stranger leaning on my Jeep in the parking lot next to my house. I mentally retraced my steps to try to remember if I locked my door. I glanced into my purse and saw my keys on top, which told me that I had. I was tempted to skip my class and return to confront the man but I couldn't find the nerve. I stood balanced on the curb for what seemed like an eternity. A trolley finally zipped past and startled me from my trance. I glanced at my watch and turned around to finish my jog toward class.

I tiptoed into the small classroom and made my way to the last remaining seat in the back row. Between the running and the shock, I couldn't seem to catch my breath. Sweat poured down my face and into my eyes. I was desperately trying to pull myself together and pay attention but I couldn't get my mind away from the image of that man. How did he know that the Jeep was mine? Did he know it was mine or was he just leaning—it was the only car in the parking lot. I told myself that he wasn't after me, that he only wanted to lean while he smoked. Why did I stop and turn around? I couldn't remember what it was that made me look and suddenly my hands were shaking.

"Gray." A whisper came from the guy seated next to me. "Gray? Are you okay?"

I snapped back to reality when I realized it was my name he was repeating. "I'm fine, Kevin, thanks." I put my hands in my lap and stared straight ahead.

"Gray, your nose is bleeding."

I rubbed my face and glanced at my hand—there was a lot of blood. Suddenly I felt weak. "Kevin." I whispered louder than I thought and I felt the entire class turn and stare. "Kevin, get me out of here."

He immediately stood and tossed his books and mine into his backpack. I felt him pull me up by my right arm and he grabbed my purse as he pushed me toward the door. "Excuse us Dr. Marks, Gray isn't feeling well." He was practically dragging me as we entered the hallway. I had known Kevin for two years—we worked together at the campus bookstore. I had a big crush on him for a time and was more crushed when I found out he was gay. I wasn't sure if I should tell him about the stranger in my parking lot. I didn't know him well enough to involve him in my problems and the last thing I needed was someone to make a bigger deal out of the situation than it was.

"Are you okay?" He handed me a damp paper towel as I rested my back against the cool water fountain.

"I'm fine. I've had a sinus infection all weekend." I lied.

"That explains the fever. Maybe you should go to the clinic. You're sweating like a pig."

"I'm fine. I think I just need to rest." I pulled myself to my feet.

"Well, let me walk you home. Are you still on the corner?"

"No." The image of the stranger rushed to my head. "I mean, I am still on the corner but I don't want to go home. Can I go to your apartment?"

"Sure." He held out his arm for support. "Is everything okay at your house? I thought you lived alone now."

"I do live alone. The landlord is supposed to bring the exterminator over today. I don't think I can handle the fumes."

"Okay. Well, *mi casa es su casa*. My place is a little messy but pesticide free. You can stay all night if you want."

"That won't be necessary but I appreciate the offer." I already knew that I would be faking sleep long enough to spend the night at Kevin's. I also knew that I had to go home sooner or later. I hoped that twenty-four hours was long enough to make the guy decide to stalk someone else. I felt a little better knowing that I didn't have to face him but the sick feeling remained in my stomach until I was safely locked inside Kevin's studio apartment.

I made myself a nest on his itchy plaid sofa. He fixed me a tray of crackers, soup and Sprite. I was feeling guilty about faking illness but appreciated the attention. It had been years since anyone had taken care of me. I tried to remember the last time someone made me soup and I figured it had been my mother at least five years prior.

"Do you need anything from home? I have a class at the language building at two, I could run across the street afterward."

"I would be very grateful if you could feed my cats. I think I was in such a hurry this morning that I forgot to check their bowls."

"No problem, anything else?"

"Um, yeah. I don't actually have any cat food." I blushed and batted my eyelids.

"I can steal some from my neighbor." He threw a cracker at me. "You are a horrible pet owner. I should turn you in to the ASPCA."

"Could you grab me some jammies from the dryer? And my psychology and Spanish books from the window seat in the dining room?"

"Sure . . . I take it you plan on spending the night?"

"Is that okay? You don't have some hottie coming over do you?"

"You're the hottest thing to hit this apartment in months. Too bad you're not my type. It's great if you stay, I'll rent some movies." He loaded his backpack and headed toward the door. "And Gray, whatever it is that's upsetting you—it will be okay."

"I hope so. I appreciate all this." I blew him a kiss as he closed the door.

I nestled my head into the pillow and breathed a sigh of relief. A minute later the door bolted open and I screamed. "Holy shit! You scared the hell out of me!" I saw the startled look on Kevin's face.

"I'm sorry. A little jumpy are we? I got the cat food but I forgot to get your key."

I pulled my keys from my purse and tossed them. "Kevin, please make sure you lock the door. Double-check it, triple-check it."

He gave me the aye, aye captain and was out the door. I lay there shaking for twenty minutes then somehow managed to drift off.

I was stuck in some sort of limbo. I woke up not knowing where I was, then I remembered the morning's events and wasn't sure if it was a dream. I thought back to the last few hours and wondered if I was really asleep. I remembered seeing the man's face so vividly in my mind that I wondered if maybe he was someone I knew. It seemed odd to me that I could picture his face as clear as a bell but I did not remember seeing his face directly in the past two days. I tried to figure out if I had dreamed about him during my nap but I couldn't remember falling asleep much less what my mind had done during the slumber.

Kevin came home at around four bearing a bag of goodies. "I have movies, deli sandwiches, chips, beer and popcorn."

"Wow, you've been busy. Are my cats okay?"

"They were packing their bags to move, they said they were neglected and seemed extremely resentful."

"Well, I can't imagine they had anything to put in the bags, seeing as how I never buy them anything."

"They were loading up the stereo and a box of noodles and some lightbulbs. I stopped them and reassured them that everything would be okay."

"Was anyone there?"

"I thought you lived alone?"

"I mean did it seem like anyone had been inside . . . the landlord or exterminator?"

"Not that I could tell." He reached into his pocket. "There was a note on your door though."

My heart raced as I ripped the note from his hands. To my relief it was from a concerned classmate telling me the assignment

I missed in my noon Spanish class.

"Secret admirer?"

"I should be so lucky. Just a friend telling me what I missed in class." I crumpled the note in my sweaty palm and relaxed on the sofa.

We indulged in chick flicks and turkey sandwiches the rest of the evening and I barely thought about who was lurking in my front yard.

I fell asleep quickly after turkey and beer. Kevin promised to wake me by seven a.m. so I'd have time to go home before my nine o'clock lit class. Around three a.m., I felt someone shaking me and saying my name. I woke up in a cold sweat and found my friend seated next to me on the floor.

"Gray. Wake up, it's just a dream. It's okay, shhh, calm down."

"Oh my God, Kevin." I reached over and hugged him. "I was having the worst dream, only I don't think it was so much a dream as it was a memory."

"Suppressed memories can resurface in dreams. Was it something awful? Did someone do something to you?" He wiped my forehead with a washcloth.

"It wasn't awful. No memories of uncles or neighbors touching me in my no-no places." I laughed a little at the idea. "Now that I think about it, I do remember the whole scenario."

"What was it? Do you want to talk about it?" He pushed me upright and sat with me on the lumpy sofa.

"I remember back when I was about fourteen, my parents were going to some art gallery opening. My friend Kristen was allowed to spend the night. It was a big deal that I was allowed to be left with no babysitter and also be allowed to have a friend over."

"Fourteen is a little old for a babysitter, Gray."

"I know, but my folks didn't trust me since I once sneaked out and took their car for a joyride."

"Always the rebel. Go on." He lit a cigarette and handed it to me.

"Anyway, we were in the living room playing Uno, listening to Duran Duran and eating pizza. Right in the middle of our game, I had the weirdest feeling. I felt nauseated and dizzy. Something compelled me to look outside."

"Maybe you heard something."

"No, Kristen said she didn't hear anything. I walked to the back windows and pulled apart two slats on the miniblinds. There was a man standing on the diving board by our pool. The moon was so bright that I could see his reflection in the water. He was wearing a black coat and hat and was standing on the board—not bouncing, not moving."

"What did you do?"

"I jumped out of my skin and told Kristen. She went running to the window and looked out. She said there was no one there then she got mad at me for trying to scare her."

"Are you sure he was really there? Maybe it was a shadow from the moonlight."

"I know he was there. I felt his presence. I saw his reflection. I went back and looked again and he wasn't there but the diving board was still moving a little."

"Did you call the police or your parents?" He handed me an ashtray.

"No. We went back to our game. I figured maybe I was imagining it since my friend didn't see him. I didn't want everyone to think I was making things up. I have a pretty wild imagination, you know."

"I know. But why do you think you remembered that all of the sudden tonight? It's been what . . . ten years?"

"Because, Kevin, there was a man in black standing across from my house all day on Sunday. Then the next morning he was there, leaning on my Jeep."

"You don't think it was the same guy, do you?"

"It couldn't be." I thought for a minute. "Of course not, that would be too weird."

"Well, when I went by your house, there was no one there. No man in black, just the usual students throwing trash on your lawn."

"Did you look in the parking lot?"

"Gray, I know how you hate it when people drive your Jeep, so I didn't tell you. I had the keys and I drove it to the video store and deli. I thought it was supposed to rain and I didn't want to waste time walking. There was no one in the parking lot and nothing happened to your precious vehicle. Sorry I drove it."

"Kevin, you can drive it any time you want. I feel so much better knowing that he wasn't there. Maybe when I go home in the morning, all will be back to normal."

"You did see him, right? I mean, you don't think he was a figment of your imagination?"

"I'm pretty sure. He chain-smoked—I'll look around and see if I find any cigarette butts."

"Finding cigarette butts that close to campus is not unusual."

"Yeah, but twenty of the same brand would indicate that someone was there."

"I'll walk you home in the morning and we can take a look. Now get some sleep." He kissed me on the forehead and walked back to his bedroom. "I'll wake you at six instead of seven and we will get it all figured out. Don't worry, Gray."

"Thanks. My hero. Sure you're gay? I still have that crush, you know."

"I'd better be sure or I'm missing a great opportunity. Night."

Chapter 3

We got back to my house a little before seven. The street by the church and the parking lot were empty. We spent ten minutes inspecting the street and curb and found no cigarette butts. I was relieved that it may have been in my mind. Of course, I was also concerned that I was going insane at the age of twenty-four. Kevin followed me inside to make sure everything was okay. I made us each a cup of warm instant coffee and we sat in the kitchen watching the cats fight over the fresh bowl of food.

"I must be crazy, I was sure we would find a little Marlboro trail."

"You're not crazy, dear. What was it that my mom used to say? 'If you think you're insane, you're probably not.'" He added three piles of sugar to his coffee.

"Well, maybe I'm overworked and undernourished. I rarely

eat and between work, school and keeping this place intact, I'm busy twenty-four-seven." I heard a noise outside, a large vehicle heading past campus. "What is that?"

Kevin stood and looked out the window. "Shit, it's a street cleaner. They probably came up your street earlier. Every cigarette butt in a five block radius has been cleaned up by now."

"Now we'll never know if I've lost my mind." I felt like I was going to be sick. "You need to get to class and I need to take a shower." I stood and handed him his backpack.

"I can skip if you want me to wait for you to get cleaned up."

"No, I'm sure he's gone. For some reason I think I would know if he was near, I'd be able to feel his presence. You go ahead."

"That's kind of creepy, Gray. You want to stay at my place for awhile?" He sounded a little annoyed.

"No thanks, I appreciate it."

"Here's my cell number. You call me any time if you need me. I'll stop by the Grill tonight and check on you."

"Thanks, I'll be there from four to ten."

I hurried through my shower, skipping the repeat instruction on the shampoo bottle. I walked around the house and made sure all the windows and doors were locked and the blinds closed. I felt pretty sure that I was safe as long as I was inside. If he didn't pursue me ten years earlier, then there would be no reason for him to try now. He wouldn't know if I was armed, which as a pacifist, I wasn't. He wouldn't know that I lived alone unless he had been watching me for longer than the last two days. I decided that I would be cautious the rest of the week then maybe I would invite some friends up to stay the weekend.

I looked out the front window before leaving for class. I didn't see anything unusual and tiptoed through the front door. As I closed the door behind me I shouted, "I'll be home early.

Call me if you need a ride, bye!" I hoped that anyone listening would assume that I had a roommate who didn't own a car. I felt pretty stupid about doing that. It occurred to me that not only was I seeing imaginary men in black but I was also making up imaginary roommates.

I found a seat in a third floor classroom of the language building. I took notes as the professor droned on about whatever book we were supposed to read that week. I made a mental note to try to read the book before Friday's test. About half an hour into class, the sick feeling returned. I felt myself get warm and checked my nose for blood. The urge to look out the window overwhelmed me and I slightly rose out of my seat to glance outside to the ground level. The classroom overlooked a different street than where I lived and I didn't expect to see him. My legs gave way as I saw the black trench coat blowing in the wind—underneath the coat, a faceless man hidden behind a newspaper. I fell back into my seat and struggled to remain calm. I stayed seated and quiet during the last twenty minutes of class but bolted for the door the second we were given permission to leave.

I ran down the stairs to the back exit of the building. I didn't care that my next class started ten minutes later—all I wanted was to get as far away from the man as possible. Going home was not possible and the safest place I could think of was the campus clinic. I bolted through the double doors that led to a little waiting area. The usual hypochondriacs were seated in tiny plastic chairs joined by a group of frat boys with legitimate colds. I handed my school ID card to the girl behind the window.

"Reason for your visit Miss Thomas?"

I couldn't bring myself to say that I was seeing things. "Bloody noses and fever."

"Take a seat." She glanced up and saw the blood above my lip. "Um, just go on back to room B. Follow the red line."

I walked the maze of hallways and let myself into the tiny

room. I wasn't sure if I needed to undress, I sat up on the table and let my legs swing back and forth. The door slammed open and I jumped to my feet.

"Are you Grayson?"

"Yes. Gray. Gray Thomas." I was nervous but relieved to see a short blonde woman. My imagination had stretched earlier and I was sure the stalker would walk in with a clipboard.

"Okay, Gray. That's an unusual name. I'm Dr. Jane Andrews. It says here you are having nosebleeds and a fever. Oh, I see the nosebleed part is accurate. Let's check that fever." She leaned into me and stuck a large thermometer in my ear. "Hmmm, ninety-nine degrees. A little off but nothing to worry about. How do you feel? Tired, headaches?"

"I feel pretty good. A little dizzy . . . and . . ." I couldn't say it.

"And?" She set her clipboard down and pulled up a chair.

"And I think I've been seeing things. Like a ghost, like someone who isn't there but I see him."

"Okay. Tell me, Gray, what's a normal day like for you?"

"Pretty average. I'm a senior and only taking twelve hours. I work a few nights a week at the Maple Street Grill."

"Mmmm. Best martinis in town. I go there often. What else?"

"That's pretty much it. Most of my friends have moved on. I live alone."

"Have you had any added stress lately? Like a breakup with a boyfriend, money problems, family worries?"

"Nothing out of the ordinary. My boyfriend and I broke up over a year ago. I haven't gone out with anyone since. My family is the same as always. I have money worries but so do the other ten thousand students at this school. I get by and have enough to have some fun once in awhile."

"Any family history of illness?"

"My grandfather had diabetes. My great aunt had heart

disease." I couldn't think of anything else.

"How about mental illness?" She stared at me.

"None that I know of."

"You might inquire. It's always good to know what other members of your family have dealt with. It makes our jobs as doctors easier if we know a patient's history. What about drugs and alcohol?"

"Maybe later. I have to work tonight." I smiled. She laughed. "Again, like the ten thousand other kids, I drink. Nothing major, just beer a couple nights a week at most. I smoked pot a time or two but not in months. I've never touched anything stronger."

"Okay. I don't think we have anything to worry about here." She glanced at her notes. "You are a bit thin. You aren't having any food issues, bulimia, et cetera?"

"I don't eat as well as I should. I eat when I'm hungry and I usually can't afford to splurge on steak dinners."

"I'd like to see you gain a few pounds. I'm going to send you home. I want you to take a few days off from classes and work. If you still have problems by Friday, I want you to come back and we will run some tests."

"Okay." I knew there was no way I could afford to miss work, but a few days away from classes was fine with me. "What kind of tests?"

"Nothing to worry about. I just want to make sure everything in your noggin is where it should be. It might be a good idea to have you talk to someone in the meantime."

"A shrink?" I had to laugh. My mother would disown me if I saw a shrink. She thought they were as shady as chiropractors. "I couldn't afford it."

"I think it might be a good idea if you can find a way to swing it. If you find the means, give me a call and I can give you a referral."

"Thanks Dr. Andrews." I held out my hand.

"You're very welcome." She winked and I felt a little more at peace.

I gave my schedule to the girl in the front office. She said she would let my teachers know to excuse me the rest of the week. There was no place I had to be until four and I didn't want to go home. I walked to the student union to call my mother.

"Thomas Gallery." The voice on the other end instantly relaxed me.

"Mom, it's Gray. Do you have a minute?" I tried to make it sound casual.

"Sure, baby. It's a typical slow Tuesday. I've got all day. What's up?"

"Is there any history of mental illness in our family?"

"Well that's a straightforward and abrupt question." She laughed. "Let's see . . . your second cousin was institutionalized for about ten years. Your grandmother was on prozac or lithium. Oh, and I had an uncle who was either bipolar or a paranoid schizophrenic, I can't remember which. Why do you ask? You're not taking a stupid psychology class are you?"

"Why was she institutionalized?" I hoped it wasn't for having imaginary friends.

"Severe OCD. She had to do everything in sets of three, sets of three, sets of three. Get my point."

"Yeah. Funny, Mom. So no serious bats in the belfry?"

"Nope, I can't speak for your father's side. Frankly, I think his mother is nuts but he never mentioned anyone with problems. Tell me what's up Gray. I know you wouldn't call if it wasn't important."

"I think I am imagining things. I keep getting a sick feeling in my stomach then seeing things."

"Did you see a doctor? My God, Gray, maybe you had a stroke."

"I went to the clinic this morning. I'm fine. She basically told me to take the week off and eat a little more."

"You never did eat right. Maybe you're anemic. Do you need

me to wire you some money? Go get a nice dinner."

"I'm fine. I work tonight, I will order off the menu after my shift, something substantial, I promise. Mom, did I ever tell you about the man in black I saw when I was a kid?"

She thought for a minute. "Yeah, I think I remember something about that. You were nine or ten and you said he was sitting on the porch at Grandma's house. We never saw him but I'm sure it was one of her neighbors. Why?"

The sick feeling returned to my stomach. I didn't remember seeing him that far back. I was referring to the night by the pool. "No reason, I was just thinking about that the other day." My tone was unconvincing.

"Honey, don't think about things like that. It took your father and me weeks to convince you that he wasn't following you."

"What?!"

"You kept saying that you felt someone watching you. You said it was the man from Grandma's porch. We had to let you sleep in our bed forever before you stopped having nightmares. You're not having nightmares again, are you?" Out of the corner of my eye, I swore I saw something black walk past the window. "Grayson, are you there?"

"Yes, no. I'm fine, Mom. I'm not having nightmares." Was there such a thing as daymares? "I've gotta head to work. I'll see you for Mother's Day. Bye." I hung up the phone before she had a chance to respond.

I grabbed my backpack and ran outside. I figured that if he was there in the center of campus others might see him. I looked behind every tree and statue in the courtyard and didn't find any evidence of his presence. I even checked the ground for a trail of butts and came up empty.

I got to work a little early and treated myself to a chef's salad. The restaurant was slow as usual for Tuesday which gave me time to sit at the bar and do the crossword while my three tables sipped their drinks. Business never picked up and the manager cut me loose around eight. I didn't want to go home—I changed out of my uniform and went back to the bar. I ordered a shot and a beer and engrossed myself in some reality show on the TV above the bar.

"Are these seats taken?" A familiar voice came from my left.

I glanced up and saw Dr. Andrews and another woman. "Help yourself. Here for a martini?"

"You know it. Gray, this is my girlfriend, Melanie."

I took a closer look at her friend and was thrilled to see a familiar face. "Oh my God! Melanie Winters! I haven't seen you since spring break two years ago! I had no idea you were living back here." I practically fell over myself reaching for a hug.

"I moved back a few months ago to be with Jane." She returned the hug.

"I had no idea you were gay, Mel." The look on her face made me think about my remark. "I'm sorry, I hope that didn't seem abrupt. I think it's great, really. As they say, some of my best friends are gay. It's just that last time I saw you, you were with . . ."

"Yes, Gray. I remember quite well who I was with." Melanie interrupted and made a head gesture toward her mate. "I also remember who you were with. Let's make a deal to leave the secrets of spring break in the past."

"Oh great. Old college chums, I can't wait to hear the details." The doctor rolled her eyes. "How about if we move to that booth and order some dinner. I bet you didn't eat dinner yet." Jane pointed to a table in the corner.

"I had a salad before my shift. I'm good, beer is food." I took a sip from the chilled bottle.

"Let's just get some appetizers, if you want to partake, help yourself."

The thought of Buffalo wings did make my mouth water.

"Okay, but stay away from the shrimp. The last people who ate them were looking green when they left."

We made small talk awhile. I learned that they had been together for a year and had bought a house two blocks from my own when Mel moved up. They met at a film festival in Dallas and immediately hit it off. Melanie owned a modest furniture company selling wholesale to schools. She did pretty well for herself and the pair seemed completely well matched. I was thrilled for them and couldn't get over the excitement of finding an old friend.

Melanie and I talked about old times much to Jane's annoyance. I think the difference in their age was becoming more evident to her. I tried to redirect the conversation toward the doctor when Melanie went to the bathroom and she immediately took on the role of physician.

"You know, I told you to take the week off—that was supposed to include work too."

"I need the money, and the Grill is shorthanded as it is. I didn't want to leave them in the lurch." I ordered another round of drinks and was relieved when the bartender said they were on the house.

"Please try to get some good sleep. Don't sit up here and drink every night."

"I won't. It's cheaper to drink at home anyway. I called my mom and asked her about the mental illness."

"Good. I'm sure that was a phone call that'll make a mother freak out. What did she say?"

"She said there was some depression, some OCD, maybe bipolar but nothing too insane."

"Well, that's good. That should set your mind at ease a little." Jane fanned my smoke away from her face.

"Uh-huh." I crushed out the cigarette and looked toward the

door.

"Uh-huh? I sense that something about that conversation is bothering you."

"Why do you say that?" My voice did the defensive squeak.

"It's my job to know when someone isn't telling me everything. I know I shouldn't pry, but a friend of Mel's is a friend of mine. I'd like to help you if I can."

I sipped my drink and debated whether or not I should confide in a perfect stranger. She seemed nice enough and was obviously concerned—or at least curious. "She told me that when I was a kid I thought I was being followed by a man in a black coat."

"That's not so crazy. Most kids think the boogeyman is after them." Jane tried to comfort me.

"When I was a teenager, I remember seeing the same man in my backyard."

"Something might have sparked the memory of what you thought you saw as a child."

"That's true." I grew silent and felt her staring at me, waiting for more. Melanie returned from the bathroom and sat next to me.

"Gray, nothing you tell us will leave this table. I could tell today that you were distraught. You said most of your friends were gone, and frankly, Melanie and I are always looking for a new friend, especially one she already shares great memories with. Plus it doesn't hurt that you can get us free drinks." She laughed and motioned for another round.

"You're both employed, you can afford your drinks. Why would you want to be friends with a screwed up, financially challenged straight woman?" I started to pity myself.

"Drinks taste better when they are free. We happen to like screwed up women, straight or gay. Most of the women we know have some sort of issues," Melanie added, although not knowing what Jane and I were talking about.

"Okay. I saw him again." I was too embarrassed to make eye

contact.

"The boogeyman? The man in the black coat?" Jane asked and stared at Mel.

"Yes." I pulled a cigarette from my pack and was surprised to see Melanie reach to light it. I went on to tell them the story of the past three days. They asked questions and seemed a bit weirded out by the whole thing. I didn't regret telling them but I could feel that they doubted my sanity.

"What's bothering me, Gray, is the fact that you are having a physical reaction to this. You said that you can feel his presence, that you get dizzy and nauseated. You've even had a bloody nose after each episode."

"Just twice. My nose didn't bleed on Sunday." I wasn't sure if that fact would help solve the puzzle.

"If you got sick after you saw him, I would say hey, he scares you and your body reacts. But since you feel sick and then see him, well I would have to submit that he possibly is a figment of your imagination." Jane cringed a little, obviously fearing my reaction to her accusation.

"I keep thinking about a theory we were studying in logic class. If A equals B and B equals C, then A equals C. If I see the man, then I'm not crazy. If I'm not crazy, then he is real. If I see the man, then he is real."

"Those aren't necessarily the factors I would plug into that equation but I am glad to see that you are trying to find a logical explanation to your worries." Jane's voice was very soothing. I could see why my old friend liked her. "I would feel better if we went ahead and ran some tests. I won't sleep well until I am sure that the dizziness and nosebleeds aren't related to the possible hallucination. I'm off tomorrow, can you meet me at the hospital at nine?"

"Stroke?"

"I wouldn't jump to that conclusion but I would like to be sure."

We stayed and chatted for another hour. By the end of the evening, I felt better about things and assured myself that there was no boogeyman following me. The couple walked me home since I was on their way. I was relieved that the man wasn't waiting by my front door but part of me wished they had seen him too.

"Okay, lady. I will see you at nine. Do you know where the hospital is?" Jane asked.

"By the mall?"

"That's the one. Come to suite four-twenty and wait by the door."

"Thanks for everything. I'm so glad to see you again, Mel. I hope we will stay in touch this time . . ." I gave them hugs and felt safer than I had all day. "Goodnight." I walked inside.

Melanie and Jane stood on my porch until they were sure I was safely locked inside. I could overhear them through the door.

"Jane, what brand of cigarettes was Gray smoking tonight?"

"Marlboro Lights."

"Are you sure?" Melanie's voice shook.

"Positive. I used to smoke them. The box was white with gold on it. Why?"

Melanie pointed to a pile of cigarette butts on the cement by my porch swing. "Because I can tell by the color of the filter . . . those are Marlboro Reds."

"Holy shit. Should we take her home with us?"

"No, we got her calmed down. Let's clean up those butts and tomorrow we can call the police."

"Are you sure? What if something happens tonight?"

"He's been following her for fourteen years, he's not going to do anything tonight."

I appreciated their concern, but part of me wished they had taken me home. It took me hours to finally fall to sleep.

Chapter 4

My cats had me up at dawn. They didn't understand the concept of taking some time off to rest because they never did much else but rest. I felt pretty good except for a little hangover headache. I wasn't sure what to do with myself since I didn't have to get ready for a quiz in logic. I remembered my promise to meet Jane at nine as well as my promise to eat better. I took a quick shower and made a grocery list. I had decided to use my parents' credit card on this trip to the Piggly Wiggly and I added a few luxuries to the list like real creamer and non-generic aspirin.

I didn't give it a second thought as I danced down my steps and headed toward the parking lot. It wasn't until I was in my Jeep that I even thought to look around. Part of me knew he wasn't there—my stomach would have reminded me before my brain did. I checked the rearview mirror constantly during the two-mile drive to the grocery store. I enjoyed myself as I walked up and down the aisles, picking out cereal and a ten-pound bag of cat food. I pushed my loaded cart past the frozen foods and into the produce section. As I rounded the corner, I felt it—the same feeling that brought the taste of bile to my mouth. I leaned on my cart, mindlessly grabbing a bag of salad and some oranges. I forced my heavy legs to carry me through the check-out line and to my car.

I knew I had to go home and unload my frozen foods and feed the cats. Although I never saw him at the store, I knew he was there. I felt that if I hurried, he perhaps wouldn't be able to keep up with me and I could get inside before he made it back to my neighborhood. I was amazed I didn't get a speeding ticket—going fifty on residential streets. I pulled the Jeep into my front yard and practically threw the bags through the front door. After the cats were fed and the groceries were put away, I felt better. I took the time to brew a pot of coffee and check my e-mail. At 8:30 I dashed through the front door, hopped in my Jeep like a race car driver and started the engine.

As I drove off the grass and popped down the curb, the man in black walked in front of me. I had to slam on my brakes to avoid running him over. Part of me wished I had hit him and gotten it over with. He stood there in front of me and didn't move, much like a deer caught in the headlights. I sat in terror and waited for him to move. He lifted his hat, like an old gentleman and revealed a head of silver hair. Then he pulled his coat tight and walked off. I was stunned to see his face, his eyes, his hands and all I could think of was how polite he was to tip his hat.

I felt a sense of peace on my drive to the hospital. I felt that I had looked fear in the face and survived. I almost turned around and went home thinking that I knew for sure he was real. Then I thought about my symptoms at the Piggly Wiggly and continued my trek to meet Jane.

"Damn it, Gray." She reached into her purse and handed me

a tissue. "Didn't you know your nose was bleeding?"

I looked down at my blood-spotted shirt and smiled. "I guess it never occurred to me to check."

"Okay, I just need you to fill out these forms. Do you have insurance?"

"Yes, on my parents' policy."

"Good. Sit over there, I'll come get you in a bit. Do you know what a CAT scan is?"

"Yup. You'll slice up my brain and take pictures." I smiled.

"Close enough. Did you eat?"

"No, but I did go to the grocery store."

"My God, you are a high-maintenance woman. Anything else happen this morning?"

"Not really. Oh, I did almost run over a man in a black trench coat. He even tipped his hat."

"You know what he looks like? You can identify him?"

"Hello . . . how many men are wearing heavy coats this time of year? He's not too hard to spot."

"I'll be back. Stay there like a good girl." She patted my head.

I spent the morning being prodded and poked. I was surprised at the number of tests they could run on one person and I told them that they were wasting their time. Aside from a few hangovers, I had never been sick a day in my life. That concerned them even more. Go figure. Jane stood by my side the entire morning which both embarrassed me and made me feel like a child. I kept telling her to leave but she insisted on staying, saying that Melanie would kill her if she left her old friend unattended. I think my health intrigued her. I finally gave in and was happy that she stayed. By noon, I was starving and they finally let me go. Jane walked me to the parking lot.

"Where are you going now?" She brushed a hair off my shirt

and I couldn't help but laugh.

"Jane, stop fretting over me. I think I'll go home and watch TV." I thought about it. "Oh, shit, I don't have TV anymore. I guess I'll go home and read."

"I want you to go over to my house and talk to Melanie. She's waiting for you."

"So the tests were all clear and now you don't trust me to be alone? You think I'm crazy, don't you. I told you I saw his face. He's real!"

"Don't get upset, Gray. Honestly, we believe you. Yes, all the tests are clear, I would feel better if you talked to someone. Go to my house, have some lunch with my girlfriend and don't argue." She was visibly annoyed. "Sometimes hanging out with a friend can be very cathartic."

"I'm sorry, Jane. You're right, I could use a few laughs and a trip down memory lane. Carroll Street?"

"Locust Street. The Victorian with blue shutters."

"Oh, I love that house. Good for you." I gave her an awkward hug and got in my Jeep.

I decided that shopping would be cathartic as well, so I took a little detour to the mall and treated myself to a new pair of sneakers. The more I thought about the situation, the dumber I felt. I had had thousands of dollars of tests run on me for no reason. I had involved and worried a stranger and inconvenienced Kevin. Kevin. I remembered he was supposed to come by the Grill during my Tuesday shift. My imagination ran wild and I raced home to find his cell number.

"This is Kevin, leave a message. *Beeep.*"

"Kevin, it's Gray. I just wanted to thank you for everything. Please give me a call." Then I started to feel dizzy and decided I had to leave the house. I pulled Jane's card from my purse. "You can reach me at this number if I don't answer at the house." I left the number and cursed myself for not having a cell phone of my own.

I drove the two blocks because I didn't want to leave my beloved vehicle unattended. When I arrived on the couple's doorstep, I was greeted with open arms.

"I was worried. Jane said you left hours ago."

"I stopped for new sneakers." I held up my foot to model the new shoes and felt like a child for the second time in one day.

"Very nice, classics." She led me in the house. "Did you eat? I have some macaroni and cheese fresh out of the oven."

"You two and your food. I would love some." I set my bag on the floor and was greeted by a fat dog.

"That's Fletch. If you ignore him, he will go away. If you pet him at all, he will follow you, become your best friend and never leave your side."

"Ah, much like his owners?" I laughed.

"He learned from his masters."

After lunch, Melanie showed me the guest room and offered me a chance to nap. I declined and asked if I could watch TV, explaining how it had been weeks since I had sat and stared at the idiot box. She joined me in the den with a pitcher of iced tea and some cookies.

"More food. I will be fattened up in no time. You guys aren't planning to eat me, are you?" I immediately realized my double entendre regarding their sexuality and blushed.

"No, nothing like that. Gray, I hope you don't feel weird about finding out that one of your good friends is gay. I have always had the feelings but I swear I never gave you a second look."

"Really? What's wrong with me?" I felt a little disappointment that she never lusted after me.

"Nothing's wrong with you. I just don't get crushes on straight girls."

"That's me. Gray the straight girl." I sighed and think I gave the impression that she should change the subject.

"You know, I've never asked you where your name comes from?"

"It's short for Grayson. It was my mother's maiden name and it broke her heart to part with it when she married my father. So when I was born, she found a way to get the name back in the family. There are no sons to carry on the name—I'm the last Grayson."

"Are your parents still married?"

"They are. I think for about thirty-five years."

"Are you the only child?"

"I am. They tell everyone that I was such a handful that they couldn't stand another."

"Well, you are a bit of a handful. You have been as long as I've known you." Melanie grinned. "Was your mother close to her parents? She liked the name so I assume she was."

"She was very close to my grandma. My grandfather died when my mom was six and she never got to know him."

"And do they live near each other now?"

"No. My grandmother passed away a long time ago. I think I was ten at the time, I remember the—" I was floored when I realized that the last time I saw her was the day I saw the man on her porch.

"You remember what?" She leaned in close, trying to read me.

"I haven't heard from my friend Kevin." I stared at the TV and spoke in monotone.

"He's the one who helped you on Monday, right?"

"Yeah. I haven't heard from him. He was at my house Tuesday morning. He said he would come see me at the Grill Tuesday night. He never showed."

"Maybe he's been busy. You know how men are. They see one pitcher of beer and disappear for a three-day bender."

"Kevin's gay. You know how loyal and sweet they are. He was very worried about me, he would have at least called."

"Gray, I'm curious. What made you think of Kevin when you were talking about your grandmother?"

"The last time I saw Grandma was the same day I saw the man on her porch. The last time I saw Kevin I saw the same man."

"You don't think he's involved in your grandma's death, do you?"

"She died of a stroke. Maybe he's the Grim Reaper."

"You didn't tell Jane that a relative had a stroke."

"I didn't think it was like a genetic disease or anything. What do you think of my Grim Reaper theory?"

She took a deep breath and sighed. "You know, I think anything is possible. You saw the man again as a teenager. Your friend was there with you. Did she die? Did you see her again after that day?"

"Yes, we double-dated on prom night. I think she went to Yale."

"There you go. If someone died every time you saw him, then your friend would have died too. We can scour the town looking for Kevin tonight if you don't hear from him soon."

"You just psychoanalyzed me didn't you?" I threw a cookie at her.

"Something like that. Did you find this session useful?" She laughed.

"I believe I did. Please add it to my tab. I will return the favor when I am gainfully employed."

"Yeah, I'm pretty good for a furniture vendor. Psychology was my minor though. What is it that you are studying now? Last I saw you it was still undecided, I believe."

"I've finally settled on a major. I'm studying the paranormal."

"Oh . . . well . . ."

"I'm kidding. My major is English, my minor is Spanish."

"And what would you like to do? Teach? Write?"

"Speak English and Spanish. That's as far as my aspirations go at this point."

"Well, maybe we can work on that during our next session."

She laughed. "Why don't you watch a little TV while I do a few chores. Jane will be back at six, we can go to dinner or something."

"Damn. Again with the food. Are you sure you're—"

"Trust me, Gray. I can say with certainty that no one in this house is going to get eaten."

"Wow, that sounds like a personal problem. Maybe we should discuss that as well in our next session." I winked and grabbed the remote.

There was a long hallway at the top of the stairs. I walked down the hall for what seemed like hours and found no doors. I heard someone calling my name and every time I stopped walking, the voice ceased. I continued down the hall and listened as my name was shouted over and over again. I could not recognize the voice—a booming tenor that almost sounded like church bells. The hall was filled with fresh flowers in antique vases and stained glass lamps. Finally, I reached the end of the hall. I was out of breath and the 'Gray bells' were gone.

I turned around and looked back to where I began. The hall seemed even longer but this time there was one door. I raced as fast as I could to get to the door, then stopped in front of it. I put my ear to the door and heard my name faintly whispered. I checked the knob and the door was unlocked. I slowly let myself in. The room was dark except for a small trail of sunlight peeking through thick velvet curtains. I dragged myself to the window and pulled open the curtains. There before me was a huge oak tree. Tied to the tree was a wooden swing—no one was on it but it was moving as though someone had recently abandoned their perch.

My legs went weak and I fell to the ground. I felt someone come up behind me and place their arms around my waist. I tried to turn to see who it was—their scent was familiar like potpourri and vanilla. I tried to speak but nothing came. I could taste the blood and it rolled into my mouth and onto my tongue. I felt the urge to look out the window again but the force around my waist was too strong and held me back. I cried as the vivid taste of blood, smell of vanilla and sound of my own name overwhelmed me. I couldn't do anything else but cry.

Chapter 5

I found myself in an unfamiliar room. I remembered I was at Jane and Melanie's house but when I awoke I was not in their den nor in the guest room. I looked around and found Fletch on the floor next to the bed licking his balls.

"Because you can?" I asked, expecting a response.

I stayed where I was because I didn't know where else to go. I thought about calling out for assistance but I wasn't sure if I would disturb Melanie who worked out of her home office. I certainly didn't want to interrupt her career. I lay there waiting for someone to come to me. I heard voices in the next room, both male and female. I recognized Jane's and Melanie's but the men's voices belonged to no one I knew. I glanced down to see that I was in my own pajama bottoms and someone else's sweatshirt. My mind raced to the evening before trying to remember if we went out, if I got drunk and allowed them to have their way with me. I laughed at the thought even though I did find it a bit erotic.

"Good, you're awake. You gave us quite a scare last night." Jane came through the door with a tray of coffee and bagels.

"What happened? What time is it?" I saw a clock but couldn't focus on the numbers.

"It's almost nine."

"Don't you people ever work? Don't you need to be on campus?"

"I took the day off. So did Melanie. How do you feel?" She placed her hand on my wrist and looked at her watch.

"Are you taking my pulse? I feel fine. Jane, tell me what happened." I was almost in tears from the concern in her eyes.

"I got home around six last night. You were asleep by the TV in the den. We decided not to wake you so we ordered a pizza and watched a movie."

"Oh, bummer. What movie did I miss?"

"Um, I think it was called *Boiler Room*. Ever seen it?"

"Oh yeah, I love that Giovanni guy. Anyway, I slept through a movie and pizza. Were you in the den?"

"Yes, we sat on the floor and had a carpet picnic while you snored away on the sofa behind us."

"Sorry about that. Don't you love the way I took over your lives?" I was a bit disappointed to know that I missed a night with my old friend and her mate.

"We don't mind at all. Anyway, around ten you started breathing funny like you were out of breath. I tried to wake you, we both tried calling your name but you wouldn't respond."

I vaguely remembered my dream. "Did I say anything?"

"No, you looked like you were trying to say something but you never did. You were sweating like crazy and I took your temperature. You didn't have a fever. Your nose started bleeding again. I tried the old towel under the lip thing and the blood didn't stop."

"Was it in my mouth?" I remembered the taste of blood.

"A little maybe. Melanie cleaned you up pretty good. She sat on the sofa with you and held your head in her lap. The nosebleed slowed down once your head was properly propped."

"Were you jealous? Huh, huh?" I waggled my eyebrows. I wasn't sure how to approach the situation. I settled on sex humor.

"I was more concerned than anything. I've never seen anyone sleep that deeply before." There was nothing but seriousness in her tone. "I thought about calling an ambulance but you calmed down after about half an hour. Your breathing was normal and the bleeding stopped. Then we carried you to the guest room. We took turns checking on you over the next few hours. At around four, I walked in and found you staring out the window. I asked you if you were okay, you told me to shush."

"I don't remember that." I closed my eyes and searched my brain.

"I think you were still sleeping. You told me he was out there. I asked who, knowing it was the man in black, but I wanted to see if in your dreams he had a name."

"What did I say?"

"You said 'Seth.' You said 'Seth is on the swing.'"

"Is there a swing in your yard?"

"No, no swing. I brought you back here to our room and left you with Melanie. I took Fletch and a flashlight and walked over to your house."

I was afraid to ask but I had to know. "Was he there?" I whispered.

"Gray, I didn't see anyone there—but your porch swing was moving. It was a little windy outside, that might have been why." She started to speak again but stopped.

"C'mon. No stopping now. I want to hear it."

"When we walked you home the other night, we found a pile

of cigarettes by the swing."

I didn't tell her that I had overheard their conversation that night. "Mel and I cleaned them up. When I went back last night . . . well, early this morning, there were butts by the swing. One of them was still hot. Fletch and I ran home and called the police. We got your keys from your purse and I met them back at the house. We went in and found nothing but hungry cats."

"Did you feed them?" I thought of my poor neglected animals.

"Yes, I fed them and changed the litter box. You should try it once in a while, they seem to appreciate it."

"I've had a lot on my mind." I felt sleepy again and closed my eyes.

"Stay with me, Gray. The police are in the kitchen and need to ask you some questions."

"You guys haven't slept then?" The guilt was setting in.

"We took turns sleeping until four. I'm a doctor, I got used to lack of sleep a long time ago. Melanie's a night owl. You probably know that as well as anyone."

"Yeah. I do remember that about her." I smiled at the memory and eased myself to the edge of the bed and forced my body to move. I felt a little sore like I had been in a car wreck but stronger than I expected. Jane helped me into a pair of jeans and my new sneakers and loaned me a baseball cap to cover my mangled hair. We went into the kitchen where Melanie was sitting with two police officers. A box of donuts sat on the table and I resisted any obvious jokes.

"I'm Grayson Thomas." I held out my hand.

"Officer Craig, Officer Daniels." The taller one motioned toward the other. "Miss Thomas, could you give us a description of the man that you think is stalking you?"

My mind drew a blank. I tried to retrace the events on Wednesday morning but nothing came to mind. "He's tall with a black coat and a black hat."

"Dr. Andrews said that you saw his face. Could you give us the details?" He reached for a donut.

"I can't. I think his hair was silver. I did see his face but for the life of me, I can't remember what he looked like."

"Anything unusual, other than the clothes? What about pants and shoes, are those black too?"

"He wears black Dockers with a cuff and black boots with a silver tip. I know he's a white guy but that's about all I can picture."

"Miss Thomas—"

"Gray." I interrupted.

"Gray. Is there anyone you can think of who might want to mess with you. Any past boyfriends?" He looked at the other two women. "Or girlfriends?"

"I'm still friends with my last boyfriend. I don't know a lot of people around here and aside from giving bad service at the Grill, I can't imagine that I've ticked anyone off."

"We couldn't find any fingerprints on the swing. We took a few from the door and windows but those are probably yours. We will check them against the prints you have on file at the college. We collected the cigarettes and can send them to a lab. Unless this guy had never been arrested for anything, it's very unlikely that we can use those to get to the bottom of this."

I let out a heavy sigh and poured a cup of coffee.

"In the meantime, Gray, I suggest you be cautious. Don't go places alone. Next time you see him, call us. Do you have a cell phone?"

"No." I remembered that I hadn't heard from Kevin. "Did my friend Kevin call?" I looked at Jane.

"He did call last night around eight. I told him you were asleep. He said he left you a message Tuesday afternoon telling you he got called in to work."

"I didn't check my messages." It occurred to me that no one knew where I was. "I should probably check them today. I am sure my mom is panicked after our last phone call."

"Well, I'm sure it's nothing to worry about." Officer Craig took another donut as they walked to the door. "Call us if you see your man in black." I saw his mouth twitch like he was fighting a smile. That's when I realized they thought I was full of shit.

"We'll keep an eye on her. You have our numbers if you find anything out." Jane rushed to my defense.

"Perfect. It could be helpful to have a campus doc looking in on you." He winked and the two men laughed.

"They think I'm nuts." I reached for a donut.

"Gray, you saw a swing in your dream and there was evidence that someone had been on your porch. If anything you're psychic." Jane tried to reassure me.

"Or a freak." I sighed and stared out the window. "I appreciate your help and I am so sorry that you had to give up your day for me. I think I will head home, do some laundry and go into work early. Jane, I'm still excused from classes this week?"

"You are excused. And if you need next week, we can talk to your professors. I would feel better if you stayed with us though. Melanie would love to catch up with you anyway."

"I just want to go home. I feel pretty foolish about this whole thing and the sooner I get back to my normal life, the better I will feel."

"We can't force you to stay but if you change your mind, come over." She handed me a key. "I want you to take my cell phone and keep it with you at all times."

"I can't take your phone. You are on call a lot, you'll need it." I pushed her hand away.

"I'll go get you one today and trade out with you tonight at the Grill."

"I can't afford a cell but thanks."

"Humor me and let us treat you to a cell phone for a few

months. Neither of us could sleep knowing that you are walking home from work at midnight with no phone."

"I'll have someone walk me home. I will take the phone and I will pay you back someday." I felt like a child once again but knew they were right.

"Maybe you should take Fletch with you. He's pretty good about barking when he hears bumps in the night." Melanie glanced toward the dog.

"I have three cats, I think it would be too much chaos."

"Again, if you change your mind, come get him."

It was clear that they weren't comfortable with my staying alone. They argued with me but I insisted everything would be okay. I tried to assure myself of that fact. Finally, after an hour of debate, warnings and coffee, they let me go home.

Chapter 6

I checked my messages the minute I arrived home. Sure enough, Kevin was fine and apologized for not making it out on Tuesday. There were three messages from my parents who sounded so concerned that I feared they were going to hop in the car and drive all the way to my town. There were also about twenty hang-ups, which I assumed to be solicitors or creditors. I figured if they wanted my money bad enough, they could leave a message. I had a wild fantasy that maybe the man in black was from the loan company and had come to repossess my Jeep. I looked in my checkbook to make sure I had made the payment and was both relieved and disappointed to see that I had.

I spent some quality time playing with my cats until I felt sure they had forgiven me for neglecting them. I had a brief conversation with both my parents, just enough to let them know I was fine, avoiding the details of the events of the last four days. I managed to squeeze in three loads of laundry and ironed all my work shirts before I had to put one on and head to the Grill. As soon as I walked in the door at work, Paul, the owner, barked orders.

"There is a ten top coming in at five and a reservation for twenty at six. Go to the basement and get the table extensions, then set up for both outside in the garden."

"Isn't it supposed to rain?" I hated working the outside tables—people tended to linger too long when the weather was nice.

"The forecast said the storms are pretty far off, I think we are safe until at least ten." Paul was addicted to the weather channel on his new satellite dish.

I went to the basement to find the table extensions. I always hated the basement in that old building—it smelled like dust and sewage. I dug around a million boxes before I found what I was looking for under a little window that opened to street level. I tried to resist the urge to look out for fear I would see silver-tipped boots. As I headed up the stairs, curiosity won and I went back down to peek through the glass. I didn't see anything but big Texas raindrops bouncing off the cracked sidewalk.

"Paul, your weather radar was wrong. It's raining." I handed him the table parts as he waited at the top of the stairs.

"Give it ten minutes, it will blow over." He seemed to have the cloud pattern memorized. I waited it out for about twenty minutes and the clouds gave way to blue skies. I set up the mammoth tables with water glasses and silverware and prepared myself for a busy night. The first group of ten was a little glee club from one of the dorms. They broke into song every time I walked by. They asked if I had any requests. I feared that I would lose my tip if I requested that they stop singing so I asked for a Beatles tune. After three choruses of "I Will," they finally threw in the towel and devoted the rest of the night to food and wine.

I couldn't figure out what sort of group made up the table of twenty. Their ages ranged from twenty-five to sixty. It seemed they weren't family and for some reason, they didn't even appear to be friends. No one talked to each other much—they ordered a lot of drinks and picked at their appetizers. They were all wearing dress clothes and seemed out of place in a college bar. I tried to be entertaining and probing at the same time. After delivering a round of drinks, I let my nosiness get the best of me.

"You guys in town for a convention?" No one responded. "Family reunion maybe?"

"Funeral." Finally, a stocky forty-year-old spoke and the others looked at him like he said too much.

Not sure how to respond, I filled their water glasses and mumbled something about condolences. The blank stares made me nervous and oddly shaky. I retreated to the bar to smoke a cigarette and sip a beer from a coffee mug.

"What's up with the gloom team on the patio, Gray?" Paul handed me a fresh mug.

"Funeral." I stared out toward them. "No one wanted to elaborate."

"Oh, I bet it's that guy who was killed in the freak accident on Sunday. I read about it in the paper. What was his name? Steve, Stan?" He reached for the folded newspaper on the bar.

My heart raced. "Seth? Was his name Seth?"

He scanned the paper. "No. Here it is, Scott." He pushed the paper across the bar and pointed.

I read the short article about a thirty-year-old homeless guy who was run over by a train.

"I thought those tracks on Allen Street were out of service."

"They are, that's why it was a freak accident. Some rich guy bought an antique train and was using those tracks to move it to his property. The route hadn't been used in twenty years and obviously Scott, who slept under that bridge, never expected them to be used again."

"Do you think those are his homeless friends outside?"

"I hope not, they've ordered a lot of drinks." He made a money motion with his fingers.

"I'd better get out there." I sipped the rest of my dainty beer and strolled to the patio.

"Another round?" I tried to sound chipper.

"Yes, and you can take the food." An older woman spoke with a raspy voice.

"Do you want some to go boxes?" If they were homeless, I hated to see the food go to waste.

"No. Just the drinks." She sounded irritated and pushed the plates in my direction.

I listened in on a few conversations while I retrieved the plates. All I could decipher was that the funeral they attended was for Scott because someone whispered his name like it was a curse word. I paused to fill a water glass and heard a woman ask the guy next to her why Scott would sleep on the tracks that one night of all nights. Apparently he had never even been in that neighborhood before. The guy said that he had no idea, that Scott left the shelter at seven and walked across town. He didn't tell anyone why he was leaving and he'd never gone out at night before. A chill ran up my spine and I hoped it was from the eeriness of the story and not the near presence of my stalker. As I waited at the bar for the tray of drinks, I felt a hand touch my shoulder. I jumped and knocked over an empty margarita glass.

"Shit, Jane. You scared the hell out of me." I was relieved to see her smiling face.

"Sorry. I said your name a few times and I guess you didn't hear me. Melanie and I are sitting over there." She motioned toward a corner table and Mel waved at me.

"I'm sorry. I've got a weird group and was thinking about their conversation." I gave her an abbreviated version of the details.

"I read about that. My friend Richard was working the ER the night they brought him in. He said it was a pretty gory scenario."

"I can't figure out who these people are. They obviously aren't family and don't seem to know each other very well."

"I recognize the lady in the striped shirt. She works at the shelter, we've attended some of the same events, if you know what I mean." She winked and I assumed she meant the lady was gay.

"Maybe they all work at the shelter?"

"Possibly. Volunteers come in all shapes and ages. Don't get too involved in the details, Gray. You've got enough ghosts on your mind without adding fodder to your imagination."

"I've got to deliver these drinks. Will you be here for a bit?"

"Yes. I've got your phone. Stop over when you get a chance."

I delivered the drinks to the table and left the check as requested. The lady in the striped shirt picked up the tab for everyone. I figured my assumption about shelter volunteers was accurate. They left about half an hour later and I found it odd that they shook hands as they exited, like they had met for the first time. I watched them walk to their various cars and no one had ridden together. They headed off in all different directions and I noticed that a few of the license plates were from out of state. My mind wandered and I made mental notes on appearances and cars, feeling the need to investigate further. Something deep inside told me that somehow Scott's death was related to Seth but I needed proof.

"Are you done for the night?" Melanie slid over to allow me in the booth.

"Yeah. I had the outside tables and we closed off the patio because rain is coming."

"Here's your phone and number. I charged it." Jane handed me a black cell phone and a card. "You have a thousand minutes and I programmed all our numbers in as well as the police and campus security."

"Thanks. I promise not to abuse it."

"I know you won't. But please do check in with us, we want to make sure that you are okay."

"I'll be fine. If you're done here, we might be able to walk home before the rain starts." I looked outside and saw lightning.

"We drove and are heading to meet some friends at the bar on Mill Street. We can drop you off or you can come with us." Melanie smiled at the idea. "It would be like old times."

"That's a gay bar, huh?"

"Yes, but they allow beautiful straight women in on Thursday nights." Jane laughed.

"I'm tempted. I would like to meet your friends and see how the queer half lives but I'm tired, my roof leaks and I need to get some pots and pans in place." I wasn't up for meeting new people. "Invite me next time when I'm not in my work clothes and I may even dance."

They drove me home and we all visually scoured the area for strangers. They waited for me to get inside and turn on some lights before they honked and drove away. I collected an arm full of pans and bowls from the kitchen and placed them strategically around the house. It was raining and I was glad I had decided to come home. I checked my answering machine and had a message from an old roommate and five or six hang ups. I turned on the radio and settled down on the sofa with a favorite novel.

About six pages into my book, I felt sleepy and debated going to bed. I lit a cigarette and reached for the TV remote. Once again I cursed myself for not paying the cable company and wondered if there was a way I could get Jane to pay for that too. I had a mental scenario of flirting with her and handing over my cable bill but realized that I was too straitlaced for the attempt. I settled back into my book and the phone rang.

"Who the hell is calling at midnight?" I looked at my watch and grabbed the cordless. "Hello?"

Silence.

"Hellooooo!" I waited and heard thunder outside and on the

other end of the line. I sat up and lifted the blinds in the front window. I looked across the street to the corner and saw a man in black using the pay phone. "Hello?" My voice shook and I got no reply. I hung up the phone and checked the lock on the door.

The phone rang again and I looked outside to see the man still on the corner. He knew I was home. I felt it was better to keep him on the phone rather than him try to come to the house. "Hello?" Silence. I covered the mouthpiece of the cordless and hit speed dial to Officer Craig on my new cell phone.

"Craig, here." He sounded abrupt.

"This is Grayson Thomas," I whispered while I stared out the window. "The man who is following me is using the pay phone across from my house."

"Gray, it's not illegal to use the phone." He seemed irritated.

"He is calling my home phone. I have him on the other line right now and he has called twice but isn't speaking."

"I'll send a car over."

"Thanks, officer." I clicked off the cell phone and went back to the cordless. "Hello, is anyone there?"

I heard the line click but saw that the man in black was still standing by the phone. I hung up and waited for him to call back. When nothing happened, I looked out the window and saw that the man was gone. When the lights of the police car approached, I decided to go outside to talk to the officers rather than have them think I was crying wolf.

"Are you Grayson Thomas?" a thin uniformed woman asked.

"Yes." I was dreading the conversation.

"We were told that you are getting prank calls from someone."

"Well, I filed a report this morning about a man who has been following me. Someone has been calling and hanging up on my answering machine and he called me twice tonight."

"How do you know it's him calling you?" She stepped under my umbrella.

"I saw him. I live right over there." I motioned to my house. "And while I was on the phone with him, I looked out the window and saw him using this pay phone."

"Did he say anything threatening on the phone?"

"He didn't say anything at all."

"Has he made any attempt to enter your house?"

"Not that I know of. I think he's been on my porch and near my car but I don't think he's tried to break in."

"Miss Thomas, there's nothing we can do. We will look around the neighborhood and if we find him we will question him. He hasn't done anything illegal yet. We couldn't arrest him unless we can prove he is stalking you."

"Has anyone else filed a report about anything similar?" I hoped maybe I wasn't the only one he was bothering.

"No reports of any stalkers. You know, the campus police do a pretty good job of patrolling these streets. If they saw anything unusual, I'm sure they'd take care of it."

"Is that your way of telling me to call them instead of you guys next time?"

"No. I'm just saying that the university keeps a pretty good watch on these houses near the school. I'm sure you are safe."

We made small talk for a bit until the other officers returned without finding anyone who fit the description. I glanced down at the curb. "Look at all these cigarettes. Obviously someone has been spending a lot of time on this phone."

"Again, it's not illegal to use the phone or smoke or even watch a pretty girl. I hate to be an ass but you can't do anything until he does something illegal. Here's my number, call me directly if he comes back tonight. I'm on duty until eight a.m." She handed me a card.

I said nothing more and walked back to my house. I watched the police cars drive off and locked the door behind me. I wanted to continue my reading but decided on sleep instead. I lingered over my nightly routine of brushing and washing, then slipped into my pajamas and headed to bed. I fluffed my pillows and crawled under the thick down comforter. As I settled in and took a deep breath, I smelled smoke. My eyes scanned the room and I froze when I saw smoke rings billowing from the dark corner by the sun porch door.

"Is that you, Seth?" My sense of calm amazed me.

"Yes, Grayson. I'm Seth." He laughed but didn't move. "You should have locked the door when you went over to talk to the cops."

Chapter 7

I wasn't sure what the etiquette was when you suddenly find a strange man lurking in the corner of your small bedroom. Part of me wanted to run from the room screaming, another part was intrigued by his presence. He didn't seem to want to harm me, he simply leaned against the wall and smoked.

"Should I be scared?" I sat up and reached for the lamp.

"Leave the light off. No, you shouldn't be scared, I am not here to hurt you." He put out his cigarette in an empty coffee cup on my dresser.

"Do I know you? I think I've seen you before."

"Everyone sees me at one time or another." He pulled a chair to the corner and sat.

"Are you a real person? Or are you in my imagination?" The question felt stupid.

"That's a tough one to answer, Grayson. Maybe I will leave that up to you to decide."

"What do you want from me?" I got out of bed and walked to the door.

"Where are you going?" He stood and sounded nervous.

"I'm getting my smokes and a beer. Do you want anything?"

"I haven't had a beer in a decade. I would love a little in a glass. Come right back though."

I went to the kitchen and grabbed several cans and a glass, a lighter, cigarettes and ashtray. When I returned, Seth was leaning back in the chair and had his feet propped on my dresser. I handed him a glass of beer and he wouldn't take it.

"Just set it there on the floor." He pointed to a spot by the chair. "Thanks."

"What do you want from me?"

"I can't say directly yet because I'm not sure you're the one I am looking for. For now, I only want to talk to you a few times."

"A few times? What does that mean? You're coming back?" I wasn't sure I could stand another minute of the man, much less any further meetings.

"We will talk tonight and every night until everything is resolved. I will never hurt you but you must swear that you tell no one of my presence or our conversations. They will not believe you, they will think you are crazy and I won't be able to complete my task." He lifted his glass and held it up to the moonlight.

"And what exactly is your task?" My voice shook.

"You will know soon enough."

"If I have proof you are here, they will believe me."

"There won't be proof of my presence. And you said yourself that you don't believe that I exist. Perhaps I am in your mind and you just poured a beer that you will drink." He set down the glass without tasting the beer.

"If I have seen you before in my life, how come you've never tried to talk to me before?"

"You weren't ready. You were too young at first then you were too clouded. Now, you are ready."

"Too clouded?"

"You have a great soul and an open mind. You are more patient and understanding than most people. For a while there, you had too much in your world and too many people around you. Now you are suitable, you are alone and you are willing."

"How do you know I am willing?"

"You poured me a beer, which I accept as an invitation to stay. You have made me welcome in your home, so I take it that you are willing to accept me and possibly my proposition."

"What are you proposing? Perhaps I am not as willing as you think."

"We will talk. If I find you to be open-minded, I will propose my plan. If you are not, I will move along—either way, you will be unharmed."

"What do I get out of this, what if I say no?"

"You get nothing. But I know you well enough, Gray. You won't say no." He spoke slowly, emphasizing every word.

I sat cross-legged on my bed and leaned against the wall. The rain had stopped and I opened a window to clear the smoke. I didn't say anything for a few minutes and the man didn't seem to care. It was as if he had all the time in the world. I tried to make out his appearance in the moonlight but all I could see was the outline of his wardrobe and hat.

"You win. I will tell no one of your existence. But you do know that I have already told a few people that I saw you."

"Including the police." He laughed.

"Right. I will pretend that you never came back, you won't harm me or bother me during the day and we will talk at night."

"I will be around during the day. You might see me but I will not approach you. You will leave this door open and I will let myself in when I deem necessary." He tapped on the sun porch door.

"Fine, but don't let my cats out and don't call me anymore."

"Deal."

"Shoot. What do you want to talk about tonight?" I lay down and rested my head on the pillow.

He didn't respond.

"Seth?" I sat up and looked to the corner.

He was gone.

The alarm clock was still buzzing and I couldn't figure out how to turn it off. Finally, my temper got the best of me and I flung it out the open window. I slowly sat up and peeked outside. It was a beautiful spring morning and the birds chirped away. I crawled to the edge of the bed and sat up on my knees for a better view of my backyard. I could see Jane and Melanie sitting on a bench. Their backs were to me so I shouted. They couldn't hear me because neither turned around.

I decided to get up to join them in the yard. I opened a door which led me to a very long hallway with no other doors. I heard my cats crying and I started a slow jog in the direction of the noise. I continued down the hall for what seemed like and eternity and couldn't find my cats. I turned around to head back to my bedroom but the door was gone. I stood frozen, not knowing what to do next. Suddenly I heard the sound of chirping birds, I ran toward the noise once again and a gray door appeared. On the door was a sign that said THE DOCTOR IS IN. I barged into the room and saw a man in a trench coat lying on a gurney. Jane was standing over him with a scalpel while Melanie was crouched and crying in the corner.

Chapter 8

I awoke to the sound of my alarm clock and the familiarity of the noise made me wonder if it had been going off for hours or if I was still dreaming. It read 10:07 and I realized the clock had been buzzing since eight. I panicked for a moment before I remembered that I was excused from classes for the week. I stared at the ceiling and tried to put together the events that took place hours earlier. I wondered if it had all been a dream, then looked to the corner and saw an empty beer glass on the floor. The stagnant smell of Marlboros convinced me that the conversation with Seth really had taken place.

I wondered if maybe I had poured the beer for myself and had drunk it like Seth suggested. I had nothing to rely on except my memory, which at that moment seemed pretty unsteady. I decided that I would move forward with my normal life and if Seth appeared, I would simply talk to him. If he never returned, then I would be fine with that too but I was curious about the whole thing.

I needed the sound of a friendly voice and called Melanie. I knew Jane would be at work but hoped Mel wasn't too busy in her home office.

"Just wanted to let you know that I'm still alive. Give me a call if you get a chance." I said into her voice mail. "Oh, It's Grayson."

I brushed my teeth and was not surprised to find dried blood on my face. It only made sense that I would have a bloody nose in the presence of my new friend. I promised myself that during our next conversation I would ask him why that seems to happen every time I see him. I stood in the shower and wondered what someone like him would want from me. What could we possibly talk about that is so important that it must be kept secret and why what I have to say would matter anyway. I was merely a college student and not a very devoted one at that. I was relieved that I didn't have to attend class and dropping out for the rest of the semester crossed my mind.

I thought I heard the phone ring as I dried my hair. I turned off the dryer three times and waited but never heard the phone. I then remembered part of my dream, the sound of birds chirping. I decided to write down the bits and pieces that I could remember and perhaps share them with Melanie. The image of her crying in the corner came to my mind, and I realized that it probably wasn't a good idea to tell her everything in my dream. I heard the phone ring, this time for real and ran down the hall, tripping over a fat cat and falling facedown on the hardwood floor. I had a hard time getting up and felt a sharp pain in my arm. I tried moving my fingers and got no response. I stood there stunned then burst into a fit of laughter—I had just broken my wrist while racing for the phone.

The answering machine picked up and I heard Melanie's

voice. "Grayson, it's Mel. Calling you back, it's almost noon. I don't have another sales call until three, so I wanted to see if you had time for lunch. I'll try your cell phone."

A minute later my cell phone rang and I followed the sound, finding it stuffed between sofa cushions.

"Hello?" I was still laughing about my arm.

"Grayson? It's Mel. You sound happy."

"Hi Melanie. Happy's not the word. Perhaps giddy."

"Okay . . . I was wondering if you had time for lunch."

"You're not going to believe this, but I just tripped over my cat and broke my fall with my arm. I think I may have broken my wrist." I was still laughing.

"Are you serious? Man, you always were a klutz."

"Yeah. Can you believe that? I'm such a dork!"

"Do you want to go get it X-rayed?" Concern colored her voice.

"I don't want to but I think I'd better. Is Jane up on campus?"

"Yes, she's working. Do you want me to take you?"

"I can't get over what an ass I am." I tried moving my fingers again. "I'm in my robe."

"Oh my. I'll be right over. Sit down and stay away from the cats."

I hung up the phone and went to the kitchen to make some coffee. Despite the pain, my body craved caffeine. I managed to do it pretty well with my right hand, and was relieved that it was the left that I had injured. I heard a knock on the front door and hollered down the hall, "It's open!"

Melanie let herself in and headed down the hall. "You shouldn't leave your door open. What about the boogeyman?"

"Oh. I think he's gone. I thought I saw him last night but it was only a shadow. I've decided that since he isn't doing anything other than smoking and staring that I would ignore him." I shot a fake smile.

"I don't know that I totally believe you but it's your life. Let me see your wrist."

I held out my arm as she felt the bone. "Move your fingers."

"I can't."

"Okay, I think you're right, it's broken. Let's get you dressed and go see Jane."

She followed me to the bedroom and commented on the cigarette smell. I pulled an outfit from the closet and suddenly felt terribly awkward about having her dress me.

"Melanie, I gotta tell you, I'm a little embarrassed about this."

"I saw you naked a dozen times on spring break alone. Get over yourself, you're not that hot. Now take off your robe." I loosened the belt and let the terrycloth fall to the floor. "Oh my. Well, we could have done that a little more discreetly." She blushed and stared at the floor.

"Make it quick." I handed her my clothes and we fumbled around until I was fully dressed, shoes and all.

"Gray, not that I looked much—but you are a little thin."

"Yes. Don't worry, I already promised Jane and my mother that I would eat more."

"And . . . well, what's with the tattoo? I don't remember you having one."

"I had it back then. You must have been too busy looking elsewhere?" I laughed.

"Is it a torch?"

"It is. A blazing torch represents immortality, everlasting life and wisdom. The opposite, an inverted torch, symbolizes death, a life extinguished. Mine, as you can see, is blazing."

"Interesting. What made you decide to get a torch? Most girls our age have a dolphin or some sort of vine. Sometimes a sorority letter."

"Honestly, Melanie, I have no idea. I liked the way it looked. I didn't even know what it meant until weeks after I got it."

"Regret it?"

"Not at all. I like what it symbolizes. What does a vine stand for? Poison ivy?"

"Everlasting itch." She laughed.

Jane was at lunch when we got to campus. We decided to wait in her office rather than see another doctor. I felt that I should give her the business even though she didn't get paid on a per patient basis. Plus I thought it might be fun to see Jane in action and Melanie was excited to have an excuse to see her girlfriend on a weekday. We found some sodas and candy bars in her mini fridge and made ourselves comfortable on her slick plastic chairs.

"Do you want me to call her?"

"Nah, they said she'll be back at one. It's a quarter to." I looked at my watch and realized how odd it was to have it on my right arm instead of my left.

"Are you in pain? I could see what's in that cabinet." She motioned to a locked door behind her.

"Oddly, I really don't feel it. It hurt at first and now it doesn't seem to hurt at all. Maybe it's not broken." I tried to move my fingers again. "But then again . . . I think these things are supposed to move."

"Want a bite of my candy? You don't like yours?"

"No thanks. I like mine but I'm fine with the soda." I stared at Melanie and thought of my dream. "Mel, what do you think it means if someone is crying in your dream?"

"I'm not a big follower of 'dreams mean something.' I think maybe dreams are simply sparked by the day's events."

"So do you think if I dream of a train and tunnel it doesn't have anything to do with sex?" I blushed, hoping I made the right reference.

"What do I know? I guess it could have to do with sex. It

could mean that things are moving too fast for you. It could mean that you want to travel. But it could also mean that you saw a train going through a tunnel earlier in the day." She sipped her soda.

"Okay. So say I saw someone crying in a dream and I didn't see anyone crying earlier in the day. What could that mean?"

"Hmm. Maybe you have sadness you aren't confronting. Maybe you are concerned about the feelings of the person who was crying. Maybe you saw that person crying a long time ago and you never forgot the image."

I tried to think back a few years and couldn't remember Melanie ever crying. "Do you think dreams can be premonitions?"

"Seeing the future?"

"Or a skewed version of what might happen." I hoped she would say no.

"I am not a believer in ESP. But . . . but you did see that swing in your dream and there was evidence that someone was on a swing."

"So it is possible that there is some sort of reality to what I see in my dreams."

"I couldn't say for sure. I'd guess you aren't predicting the future. Personally, from what I witnessed, I think anything with you is possible. I mean look at you. You broke your wrist tripping on a kitty. You are quite a character."

"That I am." I laughed.

"Want to share the dream? Who was crying?"

"Maybe another time."

At that moment, Jane stepped into her office and was thrilled to see us.

"This is a nice surprise. I wish I had known, we could have had lunch. We need to feed this starving child, Mel."

"I know. She is very thin, I just saw her naked." Melanie laughed, clearly trying to get a reaction out of Jane.

"Oh really?" Jane looked at me. "Are you here to tell me that you're stealing my girlfriend?"

"No . . ." I scrambled for a cute response but Melanie interrupted me.

"She was in her robe, tripped over her cat and broke her wrist. We are here for your professional expertise. I merely helped her get dressed."

"Oh, Lord. You are a pain in the ass, aren't you Grayson." She rolled her eyes. "Let me see."

I held out my arm. "It doesn't hurt that much. I have to work tonight, so tell me it's not broken."

She looked it over. "Sorry, kid. Let's get an X-ray to be sure. I think it's six weeks in a cast for you—and no carrying trays."

We got up to head to X-ray when a nurse shot through the door. "Dr. Andrews, there's a boy choking in the waiting room."

Jane ran down the hall while Mel and I followed, trying to stay out of the way of the hurried staff.

"He's unconscious. Get him to room one. I need a bronchoscope." Jane felt his pulse and helped lift the boy to a gurney. "He's too young to be a student. Get his parents, I need consent." Jane looked at Melanie.

"Is she talking to me?" Mel whispered.

"I think she is. I think that girl is with him, maybe she's his sister." I motioned to the door and saw Seth standing behind her.

Melanie motioned to the girl and they sat down in the waiting room. I walked toward the door to talk to Seth. I saw him walking down the hall and called after him. "Hey! Why are you here?" He never stopped. "Seth! Damn it, talk to me!" He disappeared through heavy glass doors at the front of the building and I stood still, trying to put it all in place. More time passed than I thought because when I went back into the waiting room, Jane was talking to the girl and Melanie was filling out paperwork.

"Mel, what's going on?"

"Jane got the obstruction out. It was a toy soldier lodged

sideways in his trachea. He was gone for a minute but she did CPR and brought him back. The ambulance is coming to take him to the hospital and his parents will meet him there. He should be fine." Melanie smiled at Jane with tears in her eyes. "My girlfriend saved that little boy's life."

"Yes she did." I patted Mel's arm.

"She always says that nothing major ever happens here. She complains that her job is boring and all she does is treat colds and broken bones. Today I witnessed her saving the life of a six-year-old."

"Pretty impressive." I smiled and remembered why we were there. "Think she's up for one more broken bone?"

"Oh, shit. I completely forgot. Head down to X-ray and I will wait for Jane. We'll both be down in a few." Melanie spoke while never taking her eyes off her girlfriend.

Chapter 9

My wrist was indeed broken. It wasn't a bad break but enough to warrant a plaster cast and an unnecessary prescription for pain killers. I called Paul at the bar and told him the bad news. He knew I needed money, so he took pity on me and said I could help behind the bar until the break healed. I liked the idea of not having to serve food and always wanted to be a bartender so I was grateful for his kindness, even though I knew the tips wouldn't be as good. Jane was furious that I was going to work at all but I reminded her that not everyone gets to save lives and be well compensated.

Melanie decided to treat Jane to a heroine's dinner and the two of them headed to their favorite restaurant in Dallas. I was glad that they decided not to come to the Grill for their celebration. I was proud of Jane but Melanie was getting on my nerves by rehashing the story again and again. She kept saying that if I hadn't broken my wrist, she never would have witnessed Jane's heroism. Jane insisted that it was not a big deal, that it's what doctors do, some more often than others. She said it wasn't the first life she had saved and was sure it wasn't the last.

It came to me, the part about my breaking my wrist so that Melanie could see Jane in action. It was a bit coincidental—our being there at that exact time and seeing Seth at the door. Maybe he was just following me and maybe it was a freak accident. I had always been told that there is no such thing as an accident. The term "freak accident" made me think of what Paul said about Scott the homeless guy—"he was killed in a freak accident." A child almost dying because of a toy soldier seemed a bit freakish as well. My mind tried to make a connection to all of it but it was too much for me to grasp, especially while trying to pour pitchers with one arm for thirsty grad students.

The night went pretty well. My wrist didn't hurt but lugging the cast around was exhausting. Things slowed down by ten and Paul told me to sit and rest. The Friday rush after movies or concerts was a possibility so I had a drink and waited. When things were still quiet an hour later, Paul sent me home with an extra twenty in my pocket for staying the hour. I think he was feeling sorry for me but I took the cash and kissed his cheek. If he had been twenty years younger I might have asked him to come over and have a beer but older men never appealed to me much. Besides, I knew there may be a man waiting for me at my house. I practically ran home, curiously excited about my next conversation with Seth.

When I arrived home, the house was dark and the smell of smoke absent. I called out and expected an answer like "I'm in the kitchen." Instead I was greeted only by the cats. I told them the story of Jane and the little boy. I cursed at the one who tripped me and told him that he would have to get a job to cover my lost tip money. He did not seem to care and attempted to run between my legs again. I made myself a pot of decaf and curled up on the sofa with my book. My wrist was throbbing slightly and I debated taking a pill but I didn't want to fall asleep in case Seth decided to show up. I thought about taking half but figured that would leave me half asleep and half in pain. Instead, I added a little Bailey's to my coffee and hoped that I wasn't becoming an alcoholic. It didn't take the pain away but it did make the bad coffee a little more palatable.

I read for a while then drifted to sleep. The clicking sound of a metal cigarette lighter woke me. I stretched and yawned and felt the pain shoot up my arm.

"You're late," I whispered, knowing he was behind me.

"I didn't know we had a set time," he whispered back.

"Do you want some coffee?"

"Is that your way of asking me to stay? Are you welcoming me into your home?"

"Yes, you are welcome tonight." I sat up and reached over to turn off the lamp. Somehow I knew he would stay behind me until the lights were off.

"No Irish Cream. I never could stand the stuff. Just a little sugar and some milk."

I went to the kitchen, poured the coffee into a large mug and added the milk and sugar. I returned to the living room and found him sitting on my tattered love seat. I placed the coffee on the floor next to him and went back to my place on the sofa.

"How's the wrist?"

"Broken. Why do I get the idea that you played a small role in that scenario?"

"I think it's the cat you should blame."

"How would you know that?"

"I heard you talking to them when you came home." He reached for the mug.

"If you were here, why didn't you say anything?" For some reason it didn't bother me that he had been there all along.

"I wanted to give you a chance to relax and get your mind off other things."

"So, did you play a part in my little accident?"

"We'll talk about that later."

"Okay. What would you like to talk about now?" I lit a cigarette and he slid the ashtray across the table.

"Tonight let's talk about money."

"I don't have any. If you are after money, you've stalked the wrong girl."

"I'm not after money. Are you? Do you have aspirations of being wealthy?"

"I wouldn't say wealthy. I would like to be comfortable. Like most people, I would like to have a life where I didn't worry about finances."

"Do you worry about them now?"

"I don't worry, really. I can't pay my cable bill and I obviously have to buy shitty coffee but I get by okay."

"What if you had all the money in the world; what would you do?"

"I'd help my parents, pay off my school loans and I'd travel."

"Where would you go?" He smelled the coffee and set it back down.

"Everywhere. I'd love to see Spain and Holland. I would like to take my folks to London—my dad has relatives there."

"Would you drop out of school?"

"I'm considering dropping out now. Money wouldn't make me stay, that's for sure."

"You have loans, you can't drop out now or you'll never get a good enough job to repay the debt. Besides you only have one more semester after this."

"How would you know that I'm a senior?" It bothered me that he knew so much.

"We'll talk about that later. Just do what you can to graduate. You'll be glad you did."

"Okay." I sipped my coffee and added a little more Bailey's.

"Say you could make a deal with the devil and he offered you all the money in the world, what would you be willing to give up?"

"Give up? I'd give up cigarettes or beer or laundry or tennis. Hell, I'd give up vacuuming if someone offered me a nickel."

"I mean would you give up a cat or an arm or even a friend?"

I thought for a minute. "I don't think I would give up any of those. I am very attached to all those things . . . especially my arm." I laughed. He did not.

"What about things you aren't so attached to. Like a new friend, or a toe or a hamster."

"Well, I hate hamsters, so that's a no-brainer. I suppose I could do without a toe. As far as friends go . . . I could give up a friendship if it was new but not if it did any harm to the person." I repositioned myself so I could look his way. "Is that who you work for? The devil?"

"Hardly," he laughed. "Don't worry, I'm not here to trade a million dollars for your soul."

"Do you think money is important, Seth?"

"I think that with money comes responsibility. Too many people feel that having a lot of money makes them important." He made another attempt at the coffee.

"Like the rappers who gold plate everything but their hair? Or athletes who buy car dealerships?"

"Exactly. Don't you think they go a little overboard, Gray?"

"Well, I don't know what it's like to be rich. Perhaps people feel that if they have a lot of money, they should spend it. It might be nice to have the best of everything, maybe people work hard to earn a lot of money so they can buy the best the world has to offer."

"What about the people who don't work hard, the lottery

winners or the people who got lucky in the stock market?"

"They are entitled to spend it. I don't personally see the point of having a house with forty-nine rooms but then again, I've never had the option."

"Why wouldn't you want a house that big?"

"I hate vacuuming."

"You could pay people to do that for you." He laughed.

"I have fewer than five rooms here and it makes me feel lonely. If I had a house that big, I would just be reminded of all the empty space."

"What if you had a large family?"

"Again, it's something I don't have so I couldn't imagine what it's like." I grew weary of the conversation.

"Okay, so you are not a money oriented person. You feel that you would spend enough to get by and find peace in the fact that you are comfortable and don't have to worry."

"As far as money goes, I would find peace. I don't think that true peace of mind has anything to do with finances."

"What would give you true peace of mind?"

"I don't know Seth. That's a conversation for another night." I stared in his direction wondering if he was trying to find a way to buy me.

"Are you getting tired, Grayson?" He mashed his cigarette into the full ashtray.

"I am. Is that okay?"

"It is. Are you in pain?"

"I am." I wondered if he could take the pain away.

"Take a pill and get some sleep. Prop up your arm on the back of the sofa, sleep out here. I will visit another time."

"Tomorrow night?"

"Perhaps. Not guaranteed. Don't wait up."

I reached for my prescription bottle. "'Night, Seth. Let yourself out."

He stood and walked toward the back of the house. "Oh,

Gray, I rigged your cable, you have free TV."

"Thanks, I appreciate it a lot." I didn't care that it was illegal. I wanted the company of voices in the house.

"You're welcome. 'Night."

Someone tossed me a ball and I failed to catch it. I kicked it back to them and they tried again. This time I caught the ball and taped to it was a key. I removed the tape and put the key in my pocket then tossed the ball down the hall. The hall was longer this time and there were three doors. I walked past the first door because it was red. Somehow I knew that the answer would not be behind the red door. The second door was blue and very inviting. I leaned in and listened, hearing nothing behind the door. I felt the warmth of the door and it called to me. I took the key from my pocket and tried it in the lock. The knob slightly turned and the key broke off and jammed the door. I fidgeted with it for an eternity and nothing happened I couldn't get inside and I couldn't get the key.

I surrendered and finished my trek down the hall. As I passed the third door, I noticed that it was gray. I leaned in and listened. I heard my name being called and tried to enter. The door was locked. I pounded on the door and nothing happened. I heard someone scream, "Use your key!" I panicked and cried, "The key is broken. I tried the blue door." The deep voice shouted back, "For fuck's sake, use the damned key, Gray!" I cried and fell to the ground whispering, "The key is broken . . . the key is broken . . . the key is broken."

Chapter 10

I lay staring at the ceiling wondering how long I had been awake. I felt heat coming through the window which told me that it was warm outside and no longer morning. The clock on the living room wall read 12:17 which meant that it was probably around eleven. I thought about my conversation with Seth and again wondered if it and he were for real. I saw the coffee cup on the floor by the love seat knocked over by one of the evil cats. I remembered what he said about my cable. I knew that if the TV worked it would be my sign. I grabbed the remote and turned on the little Sony. Sure enough, I was greeted with a Shakira video on MTV.

Typical of me, I was scared and exhilarated. This proved without a doubt that the man did exist. A figment of my imagination could hardly jimmy a cable box. I made an attempt to move my fingers—still no luck. My shoulder was asleep as were my legs. I tried to get up but the sharp prickles forced me back down. My perfect timing, a knock came from the door.

"Shit," I whispered, then shouted, "Who is it?"

"Gray, it's Frankie! Let me in!" My former roommate had arrived.

"Frankie, baby!" I looked out the window.

"Gray! Are your arms broken? Let me in!"

I had to laugh. "Well, actually, yes, sort of. And my legs are asleep!"

"Oh, for fuck's sake, I'll just use my damned key, Gray!" She unlocked the door and entered. "Your arm is broken?" She saw the cast. "Your arm IS broken."

The familiarity of the words scared the hell out of me—nearly the same words from my dream. I practically fell off the sofa but managed to regain my composure when I felt the safety of Frankie's hand on my shoulder.

"Baby, Gray, Gray, what the hell happened?"

"Rough sex with my Spanish professor?"

"Ummm, nope, I don't buy it." She sat next to me. "Try again."

"Rollerblading?"

"Umm. Nope, your neck would be broken too."

"I tripped on your abandoned cat and broke my wrist trying to save face."

"That I'll buy. Sorry, sweetie."

"Where's the hefty hubby and bubbly baby?"

"I got a few hours reprieve. I came up to get my transcript. I'm enrolling in medical school." She did a little dance.

"You're going to be a doctor?" I was awed.

"From the looks of it, you could use a doctor in your life." She knocked on my cast and I flinched.

"Can you get your transcript on a Saturday? Aren't they closed?"

She made a shushing sound. "Hefty Harry thinks I can. I had them mailed here, they were in your box. I wanted a day away from suburbia." She held up an envelope.

"I'm proud of you, Frankie. I think you will make a wonderful doctor." I thought about Jane and knew that Frankie would like her.

"What can I get you other than a toothbrush?"

"A cup of coffee and a bagel?"

"Let's go to brunch. Go get dressed." She stood and helped me up. "Do you need help?"

"Just a plastic bag from the kitchen to cover the cast while I shower."

She walked down the hall to get the bag. "I'm impressed that you have cable. The three of us bet that you would have it shut off by now."

"Ye of little faith." I kept the secret to myself. "I ran into an old friend who lives near here with another woman, would you mind if I asked them to join us?"

"I would love to meet your friends." She pulled the plastic over my arm. "Are they roommates?"

"Partners, lovers, girlfriends . . . whatever they're calling it these days."

"Oh, aren't you the open-minded one?" She smiled.

"Do you care that they're gay?"

"Do I care? Me? Moi? Shit Gray, I was with three women before I married Hefty Harry." She blushed.

"I know." I smiled and reached for the phone while she cleaned the spilled coffee off the floor.

"Who's the old friend anyway?"

"Melanie Winters."

"From the dorms? The girl you went to spring break with?" Frankie laughed. "She's gay? I thought you told me she had sex on the beach with that fat, sweaty frat guy."

"Apparently we don't discuss those things anymore. She was

such a nut back then. Too bad she graduated before I met you. You would have loved her. She is so straitlaced now, it's crazy. Promise you won't bring up the spring break stories that I shared with you?"

"I promise." Frankie looked a little disappointed.

We met Jane and Melanie at a little restaurant called Cozies. Frankie and Melanie hit it off immediately. I think Jane was taken aback a little by Frankie's volume and horrendous use of profanity. Jane and I listened politely as the other two interviewed each other about their lives. I learned a lot more about both Mel and Frankie than I cared to know, including their bra sizes. Eventually, Mel and I traded seats so she could be by Frankie and I could try to talk to Jane.

"You're pale." She said and felt my forehead.

"You're annoying." I said and put my hand over her mouth. "How was your night on the town?"

"We didn't make it out. I got paged and spent the bulk of the night stitching up the arm of a freshman."

"Suicide attempt?"

"No, she fell down the bleachers at the stadium and caught the corner of a rusty, rotted railing. Eighty-seven stitches and a broken bone."

"Our tuition at work—we can pay for football uniforms but we can't repair the decrepit surroundings."

"You're preaching to the choir. I get at least ten kids a year who are injured at the stadium."

"Let me ask you, Jane. If you had all the money in the world, would you donate some to the university?" I don't know why I brought it up.

"If I had an extra thousand I'd donate it to the school. Both my folks are in a nursing home, I give every penny I have to Shady Acres in Austin, Texas."

"I had no idea, I'm sorry to hear that."

"I was an afterthought. My folks were in their forties when I was born and I think part of me wanted to become a doctor so I could take care of them. My dad had a stroke sixteen years ago and my mom was diagnosed with Alzheimer's shortly after that."

"I'm sure that makes you a little concerned about your own physical destiny." I remembered what she said about our relatives.

"Aside from the martinis, I try to lead a healthy life but given my genetics, it won't make much difference."

"Do you have siblings?"

"I have an older brother who was born with autism. Of course, back in the Sixties they called it mental retardation. I have an older sister who lives in Maryland."

"Where does your brother live?"

"My sister takes care of him for the most part. Melanie and I take him a few months a year. He's a real sweetheart. My sister has four kids and he is great with them but she needs a break sometimes. She knows that I can't take him full time since I need to work to support the folks. She considers him her fifth child."

"I'd like to meet him next time he visits."

"You'd like him. He's very creative." She sipped her mimosa. "Your friend seems nice."

"My friend?" I thought she was talking about Seth.

"Frankie. She seems nice. My gaydar tells me that she plays for our team?"

"No. Well, she had her tryouts but she didn't make the team. She is married to a big man and has an adorable son named Bill."

"Well, if I had to guess, I'd say she made the team but never bothered to sign the contract." Jane winked at me and I couldn't help but agree.

"Jane, I know it's your job but I very much appreciate

everything you've done for me." I was feeling sentimental and wanted to change the subject.

"I like you, Grayson. You have soul."

It sounded strange to hear someone say that. I was relieved that Seth didn't attempt to buy my soul if something like that was possible.

"I have heard that before. Thanks." I shot a crooked smile.

"We're going to sit on the patio at Mill Street after this. Why don't you and Frankie come along."

"I don't think we have a choice." I looked at the girls across from us. "I think those two are attached at the hip already."

"Thank goodness Frankie is straight or I'd have a little competition. Well, a lot of competition—I think Mel has a crush on you."

"Nah, she doesn't get crushes on straight girls, she just likes my tattoo. Besides, you're her heroine." I took Jane's hand. "You really did save that kid. I'd kiss you if I knew what I was doing."

"Buy me a beer and we'll call it even."

"Deal."

By mid-afternoon we were settled on the patio with a pitcher of margaritas. I had never been to the bar but was impressed by the number of people there in the middle of the day.

"Think they're hiring here?" I leaned over and asked Melanie.

"You'd work in a gay bar?" She seemed surprised.

"With those eyes, she'd make a fortune here." Frankie batted her lashes. "I've never seen gray eyes before, have you?"

"Stop flirting with me, you're married." I laughed.

"Now that you mention it, I don't think I have ever seen gray eyes before." Jane fanned herself. "With the cheekbones and light brown hair, I think you would make some great tips here."

Melanie stood and motioned for someone to come over. A

short stocky woman in dark sunglasses approached the table.

"The doctor is in." She smiled and shook the hands of my friends.

"Katie, this is Frankie." She pointed at the redhead. "And this one here is Grayson."

"Nice to meet you both." She pulled a chair to the table and sat.

"Great day for indulging." She tilted her head back and took a deep breath.

"Beautiful day." Jane leaned toward Katie and whispered something in her ear.

Katie looked at me, nodded and smiled. "You need a job, Grayson?"

"Well, I work three nights a week at Maple Street Grill but wouldn't mind some extra cash on the weekends."

"When does the cast come off?"

"Six weeks." Jane interjected. "But she can function with it. It's not a bad break and she's right-handed."

"Well, I see I don't have to ask for references, you brought yours with you."

"Katie, I'm not—" I stopped and blushed.

"She's not gay," Frankie said, finishing my sentence.

"Why do I feel like I just got outed?" I laughed. "I'm not gay."

"Not a problem for me. It might be one for some of the clientele. Personally, I like the idea of hiring someone who won't spend the night flirting and going home with the customers."

"Yeah, she definitely won't give in to that temptation." Frankie sounded like she had tried with me and been shot down.

"It's not that I have anything against lesbians, it's that I don't—"

Katie interrupted me. "You don't have to justify. I said the same thing about men thirty years ago. I have nothing against men, I just don't want to kiss one. We're all born a certain way, no one has to validate their circumstances, especially around here."

"Okay." I smiled.

"With the weather getting nicer we are busier on weekend afternoons. I thought about hiring another bartender anyway." Katie winked at Jane. "So want to start next Saturday?"

"That would be great."

"Come by this week sometime and I will get you some shirts. You get twenty a shift plus bar tips and a share of the waitresses' tips."

"Thank you so much, Katie." I shook her hand.

"Oh, my pleasure, Grayson. Saturday at eleven." She stood and kissed Jane and Melanie. "Thanks for bringing in your friend. She's perfect."

And that was that, I now had two jobs and wasn't sure I was going back to school. We finished our drinks and said good-bye to Jane and Melanie. Frankie had to get back to baby Bill, and I wanted to go home and watch TV. I needed time to debate the school issue as well as ponder the reality of the situation with Seth.

Chapter 11

It was a little after eight when my nose started bleeding.

"I know you're here, Seth. You might as well make yourself comfortable."

"Turn off the TV and the light." His voice was raspy.

I did as I was told but he didn't move. "Can I offer you a soda or something to eat?"

"Are you welcoming me into your home?"

"You are welcome tonight." I headed toward the kitchen.

"I would like a beer in a glass." He sat on the love seat. "A whole beer, please."

I returned with his beer and a glass of iced tea for myself. He was blowing his usual smoke rings.

"Why does my nose bleed when you are present?"

"Couldn't say."

"Kind of makes me wonder if you are here or if I'm insane. Maybe my nose bleeds and I think you are around."

"Maybe so, Grayson." It was no answer. "You were busy today."

"Not really, I've been watching TV for the last five hours."

"You got a new job."

"Oh, you were there. Why didn't my nose bleed then?"

"Couldn't say." He held his beer to the moonlight.

"I get the feeling it's more like you *won't* say."

"Maybe so, Grayson." He sipped his beer. I couldn't remember ever seeing him partake of a beverage before. "So you want to work for a dyke."

I was immediately annoyed. "No, I want to make extra cash. Money is money, I don't care about the sexual preference of the employer."

"Last night you implied that money wasn't important to you. Today you decide that it's so important that you'd take it from a dyke."

"Are you bothered that suddenly I want extra money or are you bothered that I took employment in a gay bar. Maybe you aren't comfortable following me to a gay bar two days a week?"

"I find it curious that you decided you want more money. Were you motivated by our conversation of last night?"

"No, I was motivated by the fact that I am stealing cable television service and have a car payment coming up."

"So how do you feel about the gays?" He lit a Marlboro.

"The gays?" I laughed. "Some of my best friends are *the gays*."

"Oh, I am well aware of that fact." He sounded put out.

"Is this our topic tonight? Homosexuality?"

"No, actually our topic is choice."

"Choice?"

"Yes, as in decision. The choices people make in life."

"Are you implying that homosexuality is a choice?"

"I appreciate that people may be born gay but it is their choice as to whether or not to act on it."

"So you think they choose to be different. You think it is better that they choose to stifle their passions and be miserable every day of their existence?"

"See, Gray. You are the open-minded one."

"I don't think it takes an open mind to encourage people to do what feels right to them."

"Okay, given that statement, what about pedophiles?"

"Are you comparing gays to pedophiles? If you are, you might as well leave before I kick your ass."

"I am only making the comparison based on your statement. If a woman physically loving another woman is what feels right to her, you encourage her to proceed?"

"Yes, I do." I knew where he was going with this and I knew I was screwed.

"Well, isn't it possible that someone could be born with a trait that makes them physically attracted to children? So if a man physically loving a child feels right to him, shouldn't you encourage him to proceed?"

"Well, pedophilia is sick and illegal."

"What's for you to decide what's sick? Some people feel that homosexuality is sick. In some states, I believe that certain aspects of gay sex are still illegal."

"I believe that the topic here is choice. Choice is similar to consent. A man molesting a child is hardly consensual by both parties. It's rape. Two people of the same gender having sex is a choice made by both parties. If a man forces sex on an unwilling man, then that is rape, it's illegal and it's wrong."

"You are saying that it's okay to do something that feels right to you as long as all parties involved choose to participate."

"More or less." I thought I made a good point.

"What about abortion?"

"Oh, Lord." Screwed again, I thought.

"A woman gets pregnant. She and possibly her mate have made the choice to proceed with an abortion. You said things are fine as long as all parties involved choose to participate. Does the baby choose to participate?" He took a large swallow of beer.

"First of all, it's not a baby, it's a fetus."

"That's debatable. Haven't you seen the billboards and bumper stickers all over Kansas?"

"I've never been to Kansas. The fact that abortion is legal tells us that it is as okay as owning a firearm or speaking your mind."

"But it's not consensual by all involved parties."

"A week-old fetus hardly has the capacity to make a decision about its future. Plus it would have no way of communicating its choice."

"That is very true, Gray. You mentioned firearms earlier. You do feel everyone does deserve the right to own a gun?"

"Moving right along, eh? I am opposed to guns."

"Opposed?"

"It's a bit of a choice thing really. Some guy on the corner has the right and chooses to buy a pistol. He gets a little drunk, a little angry or as they say, disgruntled, and goes on a shooting spree. He kills three innocent people who had no say in the matter. They did not choose to be shot, they were never asked if Joe Bob should be allowed to buy the gun."

"Like the fetus who doesn't choose to be killed?" He sighed.

"Nobody chooses death." My own remark sent a chill up my spine.

"But it is legal to own a gun and everyone knows that guns kill, therefore is it legal to kill?"

"Ah, a common logic question?"

"I thought you'd like that." He laughed.

"The thing is, Seth, people are people. Humans make decisions every day from what to have for breakfast all the way to whether or not to kill everyone at the post office. It's more a debate about morals than anything. You have to hope that people will make a choice to do what is right. There are temptations and all anyone can do is make a best effort to walk away from what may harm others."

"Kind of the do unto others credo?"

"It's not a bad way to live." I stared out the window.

We sat in silence for a bit and I retrieved two beers from the kitchen.

"What about euthanasia? He watched me set his beer on the floor. "Pour it."

I poured the Miller into his pint glass without asking why. "What about euthanasia . . . well, are we talking about animals or humans?"

"Does it make a difference?" He leaned in.

"The topic of animals is a difficult one. Earlier we discussed the right to make decisions. As far as we know, animals can't make the decision as to whether or not they want to be euthanized. If they can, they have no way of conveying their wish to humans."

"So, it is not necessarily consensual? They may not be willing to be put to sleep," he said.

I nodded.

"Nobody chooses death." Again, the statement bothered me.

I sighed. "I see a bit of a conundrum when it comes to putting animals down. If a dog is vicious or rabid or so sick that he can't function, then I totally support the idea of having him put to sleep. Then there is the question of overpopulation. Why must we kill them just because we can't find homes for them?"

"Can you afford to support every homeless animal in the world?"

"No, of course not. It is a grave shame that we must destroy the creatures that we cannot provide for. What gets me the most is that some people get more upset about things that happen to animals than they do when the same things happen to humans."

"How do you mean?" He held his fresh beer to the

moonlight.

"After the big hurricane last year, thousands of people were left stranded. There were people standing on rooftops to stay above the flood waters. We all watched this on the news and though we may have cried, many of us cried harder when we saw an old dog float by on a piece of wood."

"Why do you suppose?"

"I think it's because we feel that the animals weren't given a choice. Humans were told to evacuate, many chose to stay. Some, of course, had no means of leaving. But the animals. The dogs, cats, birds—they were left to fend for themselves."

"Even the hamsters?"

"Oh, hell . . . I even feel bad for the hamsters, Seth."

"Many times it's in the best interest to put animals to sleep. There aren't hospitals where doctors can put a golden retriever on life support and provide around-the-clock care."

"I totally agree. We don't want to see our animals suffer with pain. Euthanasia is the humane thing to do in those cases. Equally, I feel that there are times where we should be that humane with humans."

"So you think people should be allowed to commit suicide?" he asked.

"I think if someone is in horrendous pain and there is no chance of recovery, if someone is in a coma for ten years and has no possibility of brain activity . . . then yes, they have the right to die. I wouldn't consider that suicide but there are times where people must be allowed to be let go."

"Do you think the cancer patient with all the pain would choose that path?" He spoke slowly.

"I know if I was in that situation, I surely would."

"Then perhaps you are wrong about what you said earlier?"

"What did I say earlier?"

"You said, 'Nobody chooses death,'" he whispered.

With no idea how to respond, I fell silent.

"I leave you tonight with a promise that your sleep will not hold any dreams." He stood. "Talk to your doctor friend about another week away from school."

"Why?"

"You don't want to go back anyway, so what does it matter?"

"True."

"And I leave you with a final question. Did you just have a conversation about choices and morals with a silver-haired stranger? Or did you just spend three hours sorting out some internal struggle with a matter of your subconscious?" He walked to the back of the house.

I heard the porch door close as I drifted off to a dreamless sleep.

Chapter 12

I did not awaken to the sound of church bells as I did the previous Sunday. I awoke to the sound of a catfight taking place on the coffee table next to me. Apparently I had left a few bites of a turkey sandwich from last night's dinner and it took the cats until seven a.m. to discover its existence.

"Stop it or I'll break your legs!" I sat up and divided the sandwich between the two of them. The third cat sat across the room looking pathetic so I flung a piece of turkey in his direction. I stretched and gazed out the front window to see the Methodist minister sweeping the sidewalk that led to the heavy wooden doors of his majestic building. Part of me felt the urge to help the man. The part of me in the purple cast felt the urge to take a bath and read the paper. I let that part of me win and retrieved the paper from the porch.

"Good morning Miss Thomas!" the minister shouted across the street.

I was startled that he knew my name. "Oh! Morning, Minister!"

"Do you have a moment to talk?" He shouted back.

"Sure." I looked at my feet.

"You're barefoot, I'll come over there." He put down his broom and walked in my direction.

"What can I do for you?" I sat on the porch swing and patted the area next to me.

"The police told me you were having some difficulties with a stranger."

"Well, I think everything has been resolved. I'm not worried about it anymore. Why, did you see him?"

"No, I asked all the folks at the church. None of us saw anyone in a black coat recently."

"Recently?" My heart jumped hoping he meant he had seen him in the past.

"Well, I mean, lots of men wear black coats. We haven't seen anyone around lately . . . you know, since the weather has been so nice."

"Oh, yeah. That makes sense."

"Miss Thomas, do you attend services anywhere?"

"I don't. I haven't in about ten years. I went to the Episcopal church until I was about fourteen."

"Was it something he said?" The minister laughed.

"Who? God?" I laughed back.

"No." He slapped his knee and chuckled. "The priest."

"No, it was nothing like that. It's just—"

The minister interrupted me. "Miss Thomas, you don't have to explain why you don't attend services. But please feel free to drop by anytime. It doesn't even have to be on a Sunday with the rest of them. Come by and see me if you'd like. We are all in this community together, no matter what or whom we believe in."

"I appreciate that." I held out my hand.

"Ricky." He returned my handshake.

"Thank you, Ricky. I'm Grayson."

"Great to meet you. Please come by." He stood and walked away.

I felt peculiar that I thought he was kind of cute. He couldn't have been much older than thirty. I wondered if Methodist ministers were allowed to marry. I watched him go back to his sweeping and I went inside and laughed at myself.

I treated myself to a long bubble bath and listened to the bells outside. I thought about what an interesting path my life had taken over the past week. A path that led me to a medical doctor, an old friend, a priest, a new job and the dark stranger. A week ago, I was merely a college student trying to decide what to do with the rest of my life. Now, I was a woman who was having conversations with herself or so it seemed.

I decided that the best thing to do was to try to figure out if Seth was real. He mentioned an internal struggle. What could that possibly mean? I thought about calling my mother but I knew she would worry and give me nothing but motherly advice. I wondered if it would be too presumptuous to call Mel and Jane and see if they could help. I had seen them every day for the last five days. I didn't want to overwhelm them with my presence but I also didn't want to figure this out on my own.

"Melanie, it's Grayson."

"Hello, fractured friend." She sounded chipper.

"Am I calling too early?" My watch read ten minutes to nine.

"Not at all. We are up and enjoying the beautiful weather on the porch."

"Do you guys have a day planned?" I tried to sound casual.

"Not really. We were going to hang out here today, maybe grill some burgers for lunch."

"Oh, okay. Well, I wanted to check in, let you know I was not abducted."

"Gray, are you fishing for an invitation?" She laughed.

"Mel, I need to talk to someone. Would you mind if I came over?" I was embarrassed.

"Come on over. Fletch would love to see you. So would we. Are you okay?"

"Oh, yeah, I'm fine. I guess I'm just a little lonely."

"See you in ten?"

"Great." I hung up the phone and hoped I wasn't about to make an ass of myself.

I found the two ladies on their front porch eating croissants. An empty chair sat between them and Fletch was begging by Jane's side.

"Good morning." I waved my cast-free hand.

"Join us." Mel pushed the chair with her foot. "Grab some coffee and food."

"Yes, grab lots of food, you thin child." Jane laughed.

I helped myself to a croissant and a cup of coffee. It smelled so much better than the brown water I made at home.

"Melanie said you need to talk. Is this a personal conversation between friends? I could go inside." Jane started to stand.

"No, just some friendly advice. Nothing too personal. Jane, I would like to take another week off from school. Would it be possible for you to permit that?"

"Well, why don't we talk for a bit and see why you feel you need more time. It's so close to the end of the semester that I'd hate to see you miss any more classes. Some teachers will fail you if you miss more than four, excused or not."

Melanie placed her hand on my knee. "What's going on, Gray?"

I took a deep breath and tried not to cry. "I don't know. I feel a little lost or confused or scared. I don't know what is going on in my head but I think I am having a hard time distinguishing between what is real and what is imaginary."

"Do you still think that man is following you? Have you seen him again?"

I tried to think of a way to explain it to them without confessing too much. "I am at peace with his existence. I do not know if he is there or not but I am not worried that he will harm me."

The two looked at each other and neither spoke.

"What I mean is . . ." I couldn't think of a way to elaborate. "Let's say he is there, that he is a real live person. He just watches me and stuff. He has made no attempt to hurt me."

"And stuff?"

"Well, he hasn't done anything illegal."

"Okay," Jane said.

"But let's say he doesn't exist, except in my mind. What if I was having imaginary conversations with him? What if I talked to him about morals and hamsters? Does that mean I'm mentally ill?"

"Are you having conversations with him?" Melanie leaned in.

I was about to respond when my cell phone rang. I didn't have to answer it to know that it was Seth calling. I felt the trickle of blood roll from my nose. I turned off the phone and made an attempt to change the subject.

"I really appreciate the phone. Your kindness is overwhelming." I leaned over and started crying.

Jane stroked my back. "Grayson. Shhh. It's okay." She looked at Mel. "Are you talking to him?"

I thought of a new approach and sat up. "Do you think it's possible to have a problem that you don't even know exists? I guess an internal struggle but you don't know what it's about?"

"I think you are talking to two women who are very familiar with that concept," Jane answered.

"What do you mean?"

"When I was growing up, I knew I was different. I knew

that I was having problems fitting in, that I didn't feel normal or want normal things. I had no idea that I felt that way because I was gay. I was twelve years old. Why would I assume that my awkwardness had anything to do with my sexuality? At age twelve, I didn't even know what sexuality was. I spent the next decade feeling like an outsider. When my friends talked about boys, I went along with it but I never realized that was all I was doing. I was going along with the majority, the socialized self. It wasn't until I was twenty-two that I realized that it was homosexuality I was struggling with."

"So maybe there is something inside of me that I need to figure out? I know I'm not gay. I like boys too much. I was even ogling the Methodist minister this morning."

"Ricky." Jane smiled. "Ricky's kinda cute and very funny."

"You know him?"

"He's my second cousin. We have coffee every few months," Melanie bragged.

"I never knew you had family here." I smiled and moved on. "So I feel like there is something about me that needs to surface. Maybe I have missed my calling. Maybe I was supposed to be a musician or an artist or a serial rapist." I have no idea where the last thought came from and it startled me.

"Well, there are very few female serial rapists so I think you can take that off your list. You know, lots of students go through some sort of identity crisis during their senior year. It's a time where you're committing to a career and about to face the real world. People question their majors and wonder if another field might have been better for them."

"But I don't even want to be in school anymore." I was frustrated.

Melanie took my hand. "Maybe it's not that you don't want to be in school. Maybe it's that you don't want to graduate. You're afraid of finding a job and leaving the comfort of the campus and its lifestyle. Maybe you're afraid because you don't know what to do with your degree."

"You know, Mel, I am a rational, intelligent person. If I thought there was any truth to that, I would say that you're right and I would go back to class on Monday. I can tell you that something inside me is telling me to stay away a bit longer, maybe even forever." I couldn't tell them it was Seth telling me to take another week off. "I can't go back to school right now. Not until I figure out what is going on with me."

"Okay, Grayson. I am going to authorize another week off but only because your nose is bleeding again and not because I think you have mental problems. You obviously have something going on that is affecting you physically." She handed me a napkin. "You have to swear to me though, swear that you are not using cocaine or heroine or anything that may cause hallucinations and physical symptoms." She almost sounded annoyed.

"Jane, I promise that I am not taking any drugs other than the painkillers you prescribed. I have never done coke or heroine and I'd be willing to take a drug test to prove it." I tried not to sound defensive.

"You don't have to take a drug test," she said with relief. "I believe that you arc not the type of person who would be welcomed into our home, then turn around and disrespect us."

The phrase caught me off guard. "Am I welcome in your home?"

"Always. A true friend never has to ask."

Her response bewildered me. A true friend never has to ask. It made me wonder if Seth was of a friendly nature, why would he continue to ask me if he was welcome? I decided I would see what happened if I no longer welcomed him.

My friends and I spent the day grilling and talking as if we had known each other all our lives. Melanie and Jane shared stories of what they were like when they were my age. Of course it was just a few years ago for Melanie. I felt a little better about things knowing that everyone does struggle with something at times. I couldn't help but feel that my problems were a bit bigger than most. It made sense that I would think that everyone feels that way.

I rented some movies and was back home by dark. Although I felt like I had done some soul searching, I also felt that I had wasted the day. It was probably the first Sunday in years where I didn't worry about Monday classes or upcoming tests. I had no homework to do, no alarm to set and no one to call. I propped my arm on some pillows and indulged in some classic Hitchcock black-and-whites.

Between movies I went to the kitchen for some popcorn. Before I turned on the light, I saw Seth sitting at the kitchen table.

"Been here long?" I didn't turn on the light.

"Not too long." He leaned back in the chair. "Have a good day? A nice talk with Jane?"

"I did. It was a wonderful day with my friends, both Jane and Mel."

"Jane is the one I am interested in."

"Well, I can assure you that you are not her type." I laughed.

"Not like that. But that's a conversation for another night." He sighed. "Are you going to offer me a drink?"

"Nope." I stared out the window.

"Am I welcome in your home?" he asked nervously.

"No. You are not welcome in my home tonight." My voice shook.

"There will be repercussions, Gray. If we lose a night there will be consequences."

I had no idea how to respond. I stood firm in my decision. "I can live with that."

"Are you going to school tomorrow?" He stood.

"Why don't you wait and see, you follow me anyway." I wasn't backing down.

"Will you see Jane tomorrow?" He stared through me.

"No. I have no plans to see Jane or Mel." I wanted to leave them out of it. "My friendship with them does not concern you."

"You will see Jane tomorrow and you will welcome me into your home tomorrow night." He tilted his head toward the window and I caught a glimpse of his face. He was smiling. He tipped his hat and walked through the door. "Sweet dreams, Grayson Thomas."

I stood frozen, not knowing what to do next. I felt that I had done the right thing but there was no way to know for sure. I decided to remain calm and see how bad the consequences could be. I took two painkillers and fell asleep quickly in my bed.

I heard a loud crash followed by silence. I lay in bed trying to figure out the source of the noise. A few minutes later I heard the sound of sirens. I crawled out of bed and ran to the door. As I entered the hallway, I saw that the gray door at the end of the hall was wide open. I ran as fast as I could down the hall and went into the smoke-filled room. Inside I found several boxes of mechanical parts and dynamite. I paced around the room wondering what I was supposed to do.

I pulled open the drapes when I heard a knock on the window and found Jane standing on a ladder holding out a box. I tried to open the window but it was painted shut. "Break it," she screamed. I put my fist through the glass and reached out. She handed me the small box and told me to hurry. I pulled open the flaps to reveal a brand new Canon Sure Shot camera. "What am I supposed to do with this?" I held it up.

Jane didn't respond. I watched her climb down the ladder and run to Melanie. They embraced for a moment then ran down the street. I called after them but they were too far away to hear me.

The smoke in the room grew thicker and I dove to the ground. I felt my cast hit something dense and pain shot through my arm. The sirens stopped abruptly and the smoke was suddenly gone.

Chapter 13

The phone was ringing off the hook. I ran to the living room and the answering machine turned on before I was able to pick it up. I heard my cell phone ringing and couldn't find it anywhere. I followed the ringing sound and discovered that the cats had knocked it under the sofa. The home phone started ringing again and I grabbed it on the second ring.

"Grayson, oh, thank God. It's Kevin." He was out of breath.

"Hey, Kevin. What's going on?"

"You didn't hear the explosion?"

"I just woke up. I took painkillers. I've been out."

"I've been calling you nonstop for ten minutes." He was talking fast.

"Someone planted a pipe bomb in our classroom."

"What? Are you serious?" My stomach sank.

"Yes. Dr. Marks opened his desk drawer and found it. He moved fast and got everyone out of the building. They are pretty sure that no one was badly injured. A few people fell down during evacuation. It went off about ten minutes after he found it."

"Oh, my God." I was in shock.

"I wanted to make sure you weren't still in the building. I thought you might be skipping again today but I had to be sure." He started crying. "Oh, God, Gray. I was terrified when you didn't answer your phone."

"I'm okay, Kevin. I'm glad you and everyone else got out. How bad is the damage?"

"It's just that one room but they are canceling all classes at Canon Hall until they are sure it is structurally sound."

Canon Hall. Canon Hall. "Kevin, I need to let you go, I feel a little dizzy. I'll talk to you later?"

"Okay. I'll come see you at work this week." He sniffed.

I threw up right there in the living room. The word *consequences* resonated in my head. I ran to the bathroom, the retching coming on again. I leaned over the sink and looked at my pale reflection. The dark circles made my gray eyes look almost white. Pain shot up my arm and I looked down to see that my cast was broken. *You will see Jane tomorrow.*

"I'll go to the hospital," I said to my reflection. "I don't have to see Jane. I can go see a different doctor." I splashed water on my face. "Co-pay. Insurance. Bills." I sighed. "I'll duct tape it. I can wait until tomorrow. I don't have to see Jane today."

My cell phone rang—it was Paul from work. "Gray. Bobby was supposed to bartend today but he broke some ribs in the evacuation at the campus this morning. You must be a little tougher with the broken wrist." He laughed. "Can you come in at three and bartend until nine or ten?"

I started laughing hysterically. "No problem. I can be there at three."

"What's so funny?"

"Everything in my life is suddenly intertwined. It's like someone is forcing the wrong pieces together in a puzzle but somehow it's managing to stay together."

"And this is funny to you? Are you okay?"

"Oddly, I've never felt so alive. See you at three."

My duct tape idea didn't work. I was destined to follow the plan Seth set out for me and decided to go to the clinic. I hoped she would be too busy with others and I could see a different doctor. I forced down some breakfast, put layers of makeup over my dark circles and put on my work shirt. I waited until noon to go to the clinic, praying that Jane had taken a lunch break.

"Go to Room B. Follow the red lines. Dr. Andrews will be right with you." The tiny receptionist handed back my ID.

"Dr. Andrews? Is there another doctor I could see?"

"Do you have a problem with Andrews?" She reached for a pen.

"No." I didn't want to cause problems. "Room B."

I hopped up on the paper-draped table and promised myself that I wouldn't linger or have significant conversation. I would keep it short, make small talk and be done in record time. Jane came through the door looking haggard.

"Oh, fuck, Grayson. What is it now?" She didn't bother to laugh.

"My cast is coming off." I held up my arm to prove it.

She took a closer look. "What did you do to it? It looks like you took a hammer to the top."

"I just woke up with it that way."

"Must have had a crazy dream. We'll need to X-ray it again to make sure you didn't make it worse. Follow me." She opened the door with her foot.

"Crazy morning, eh?" I kicked myself for starting a conversation.

"To say the least."

"Did you get a lot of students?"

"Oh. The evacuation. Most of those kids were taken to the hospital by ambulance. We had a few walk-ins."

"Then why was your morning so crazy?" Why was I asking questions?

"I delivered a baby at the dorm." She smiled.

"What? That's a little odd."

"I know." She sighed. "I've had the weirdest cases lately, yourself included."

"There was a pregnant girl living in the dorm?"

"She swears she didn't know she was pregnant. She's an athlete, here on a track scholarship. She thought she had just gained the freshman fifteen. Said her cycle was always off anyway from running. She was more shocked than anyone."

"Wow. That's incredible. Are they both okay?"

"The baby was premature, very tiny. He wasn't breathing but I managed to get some life in him." She beamed.

"You've breathed life into two boys in a week. Melanie's gonna buy you a plaque. How is the mother?"

"She's fine. When I left she was trying to figure out how she was going to tell her parents and her track coach."

"I'd like to be a fly on the wall for that conversation."

"No shit."

She led me into the X-ray waiting area and we sat on plastic chairs. I couldn't resist telling Jane what was on my mind. Maybe I hoped she would have some words of wisdom.

"You know that classroom where they found the bomb?"

"Yeah, over there in the Canon building."

"That was my classroom. My first Monday morning class is in that room."

"Wow. Maybe you had some sort of premonition . . . maybe that's why you were telling yourself that you couldn't go back this week."

"Maybe."

"So maybe now it's safe for you to go back?" She patted my

shoulder.

"My mind is still telling me to stay away. I hope that doesn't mean anything else is going to happen on campus."

"I'm sure all will be fine. It could have been a coincidence." I didn't bother to tell her about the dream. The X-ray showed the bone to be the same, no worse than before. She replaced the cast and asked no questions when she found a few small shards of glass wedged in the bottom. She said I was fortunate that they didn't break the skin. I also didn't bother to tell her that I was working later. I didn't want them to come in for martinis. I enjoyed their company but Seth's interest in Jane disturbed me.

The bar was incredibly slow. Paul said he hadn't seen it that slow, even on a Monday, in fifteen years. Our one customer was the town drunk and he was there only because he was Paul's brother. No one even came in for happy hour and we threw in the towel and shut everything down at seven. Paul tried to give me an extra fifty for wasting my time but I declined. Something told me that somehow it was my fault that the bar was dead. It was one of the *consequences* of my actions.

Chapter 14

I walked home as slowly as I could, dreading the rest of my night. I wondered what would happen if I decided to stay at Kevin's apartment. Surely the stranger wouldn't follow me into someone else's home. He definitely wouldn't be welcomed there. I knew that I would have to pay the price if I denied conversation two nights in a row. I didn't want to imagine what could be worse than a bomb, even though no one got hurt.

When I arrived at the house, the front door was unlocked. I knew I had locked it when I left—I didn't need a nosebleed to tell me he was there. The lights were off and I knew better than to turn them on. I stumbled in and felt my way down the hall to the kitchen.

"Evening." I saw him sitting at the kitchen table.

"How was your day, dear?" He chuckled condescendingly.

"You oughtta know." I reached into the fridge for a soda, then spoke in my own condescending tone. "Can I offer you a drink?"

"Am I welcome in your home?"

"Yes, you are welcome in my home tonight," I sighed.

"I will have a beer in a can."

"I only have bottles left."

"A bottle is better, thank you."

I unscrewed the top and slammed it on the table in front of him. "It's an import. You owe me three bucks." I tried to sound serious.

"And a good import at that." He pulled a bill from his pocket and tossed it at me.

"I don't make change." I put the fifty in my jeans and sat down. "So, what's our topic for tonight?"

"Politics." He laughed.

"If you know me at all, you know I don't discuss politics with anyone. Try again."

"That's fair. Just one question? Why don't you discuss politics?"

"Because the current leader of the free world is a dill weed. I have absolutely nothing but bad things to say about the administration and I find that my views annoy a lot of people."

"Well, I don't follow politics myself but I did watch your TV a bit earlier and I would have to agree with your opinion."

"Good. We have something in common," I snapped.

"Gray, you're going to have to drop the angry woman act if you want this to work. You can't be mad at me, I warned you of the aftermath." He spoke distinctly.

"That's true. Okay, you're forgiven since no one was seriously injured."

"Okay. Tonight we will discuss religion."

"Oh, Lord." I rolled my eyes.

"Yes, him too." He laughed. "I saw you speaking to the

minister yesterday. Was he inviting you to his sermon?"

"He told me to come by the church. He said I was welcome anytime." My statement made Seth uncomfortable and it occurred to me that maybe I could use the church as a refuge. I was welcome in God's home. Was Seth?

"Are you going to go?"

"Maybe. The minister was very nice and we are all part of the community." I tried to repeat Ricky's words.

"Are you Methodist?"

"No. I was raised Episcopal." I stood in front of the fridge looking for a snack. "Oh, I think I'd like some ice cream, would you like to join me?"

"No, thanks. Not with beer. So are you still an Episcopalian?"

"I consider myself agnostic." I sat down with my bowl of vanilla.

"That's what I figured. Agnostic can mean different things to different people. How do you define your belief?"

"I believe the possibility that there is a guiding force, something leading us all. I don't necessarily believe that it's God. I see no evidence of the existence of God. I guess I'm waiting for some proof."

"What about the Bible, the stories of Jesus?"

"If I wrote a novel about a superhero and told everyone that the hero existed, does that prove that the hero existed?"

"So you are saying that the Bible is a work of fiction?"

"I have nothing to prove it's not."

"Isn't it a bit blasphemous to imply that the Bible is nothing but fabrication?"

"Blasphemous? How can I speak irreverently about God if I doubt his existence?" I thought for a moment. "That would be like saying I was disrespectful to the Easter Bunny or Santa Claus."

"But we know that those characters don't exist." He laughed.

"Do we? Who's to say they don't exist? How can we tell our five-year-old child that he must attend church every Sunday and believe in God? Then tell him he must behave so he can get gifts from Santa. We are implying that they both exist. Then eight years later, we confess that Santa doesn't exist. We expect the child to continue to believe in one man he has never seen but not the other? Frankly, I've had more Santa Claus sightings in my lifetime than sightings of God."

"Are you comparing God to Santa Claus?"

"Of course not. That would be blasphemous." I laughed. "I feel that people will believe in anything if you give them reason to. Believe in Santa, he will give you gifts. Believe in God, he will give you a path."

"Don't you think that people need a path?"

"I said earlier that I believe in the possibility of a guiding force. I think people *need* to buy into something. I view religion as a way for people to join together and share something precious to them. A female attorney, a black school teacher, a stoner bus driver, a pregnant teenager—what are they going to share? What do they all have in common? It's the community, the church brings them all together and makes them equal. No one is any smarter than the other or any richer than the other when they are sitting in church. They are all merely followers on the path together." Oddly, it almost sounded appealing to me.

"So what about people who are considered to be religious fanatics. Don't they think they are better than others?"

"It gives them the opportunity to judge people. I think the key to anything in life, including religion, is moderation. Most of the time, in my opinion, people who are religious fanatics are those who aren't wealthy or highly intelligent or creative geniuses."

"Are you saying that zealots are nothing but poor white trash?"

"Well, no. But have you ever seen a Nobel Prize winner thank God in his speech? Have you ever seen a member of Mensa lead a revival? People who worship God to the point where it rules their life seem to have nothing else to focus on. Even the wealthiest corporate CEO isn't going to credit God with his success, even though he may attend church."

"So are you saying that highly intelligent people don't believe in God?" He sipped his beer.

"They may believe in God. I don't think they see God as the driving force of their life."

"What about athletes who thank God after they win the Super Bowl?"

"I may sound like an ass, but the ones who thank God usually aren't the ones who got a four-o in college. If you know what I mean. I think they were probably educated thanks to a football scholarship rather than an academic one."

"You said the key to anything in life is moderation. How so?"

"Moderation balances everything out. If you exercise too much you could damage your body. If you don't exercise at all, you could be fat with a weak heart. If you find a middle ground, then your body will be healthy."

"Similarly, if you drink too much you could damage your body but what if you don't drink at all?" He asked and held up his empty beer bottle.

"Good question. If you enjoy alcohol and limit the use of it, I don't see why you couldn't enjoy a healthy relationship with beer. Much like if you enjoy church and control your religious enthusiasm, then religion can be a healthy part of your life. If you go overboard, you could miss out on other things and if you don't believe in anything at all, you could miss out on being a part of a community." I opened the fridge.

"But you don't believe in anything at all."

"Not true. I believe in community. I believe in helping my neighbors, being a good friend, loving those around me." I handed him another beer. "I even believe in welcoming an occasional stranger into my home—in moderation." I smiled.

"Doesn't everyone believe in community? In helping others and loving their friends?"

"I'd like to think so. There are selfish people out there. Some people find other types of community. Alcoholics have a community within AA. They are all on the same path and share similar stories and beliefs. They have a common goal and they are all equals—no one richer or smarter—when they are seated at a meeting."

"So basically you are saying that religion is being a part of a community?"

"Look around the world—there are a trillion different religions. Overall, the underlying thing that they all have in common is community. Jews get together at temple and treat one another with love and respect. Same with the Islam. They all follow the same path and ultimately have the same goal, no matter what they believe in."

"And what goal is that?"

"To share something they care about with others who care about the same things. If it wasn't for religion, there would be no common ground bringing together different ages, races, economic backgrounds, etcetera."

"But there is no church or temple for agnostics like you. Where do you get together with others and treat them with love and respect?"

"In my heart. I know it sounds corny. I treat every single person I encounter with an open mind. Whether they believe in God or not, whether they are black, white, gay, straight, stupid, smart—I treat everyone with equal respect and love."

"Even Republicans?"

I sighed. "Yes. I even respect and love the Republicans."

He leaned back in his chair and put his feet on the table. I assumed this meant we weren't finished with our conversation. I set my bowl of melted ice cream on the floor for the cats to finish. I waited for him to speak but after about ten minutes, I grew impatient.

"Seth, are we finished for tonight?"

"No, we lost a night, remember?"

"Yes." I bowed my head. "So what's next on the agenda?"

"What about fate? Do you believe in fate?"

"Fate as in things that are out of our control? Or fate as in how we will die?"

"Death is a conversation for another night."

The tone in his voice shook me. "So fate, destiny, things that are predetermined."

"Yes. Do you believe that both good things and bad things can be ruled by fate?"

"Well, it could be my destiny to be in a car accident on July eighteenth in the year twenty twenty-one. I believe that if fate exists, there is nothing I can do to change that. I could stay in bed all day but then maybe my house would catch on fire which would force me to take a car to a Red Cross shelter, at which time the car could crash. So that would be a bad thing."

"Yes." He lit a cigarette.

"It could be in the cards for me to meet a tall, blue-eyed man and have three children with him. I could avoid talking to all tall men but something would intervene and force me to meet the father of my children."

"So you believe the crash and the babies could be your destiny and nothing could change that."

"Not necessarily those scenarios specifically but I do believe that there are some things coming to us that we cannot change."

"So you believe in fate."

"Seth, I believe in everything."

"Except God."

He'd done it to me again. He'd taken my own words and found a way to make me question my own opinions. For the second time in two conversations, he left me speechless. First I said that no one chooses to die. Now I've stated that I believe in everything, except God. I did not like the direction the conversations were heading. I tried desperately to find a way to backtrack but couldn't. I tried to remain calm but I sensed that he knew I was uncomfortable.

"Thank you for the beer." He slid his empty bottle across the table. "And for the conversation."

"I'd like to say that it's my pleasure but I'm not sure I feel that way."

He stood. "I leave you tonight wishing you a dreamless sleep."

"I appreciate that."

"You will see Jane tomorrow?"

"I have no plans to. I just met her, I don't want to overwhelm her with my presence."

"Don't make me intervene." He stood over me.

"I will think of something."

"Yes, you will." He walked to the back of the house. "A few more visits and everything will fall into place."

"Should I be afraid?"

He didn't respond. I heard the back door slam shut and the house was eerily silent. I took two pain pills, more because of my desperate want of sleep than for any physical pain I felt. I was rewarded for my hospitality with a dreamless sleep as promised. I slept a solid eight hours and felt refreshed the next morning.

Chapter 15

I sat in the bathtub trying to think of a reason to visit Jane. It was evident that I was supposed to see Jane every day and Seth every night. I didn't understand why it had to be that way, but I knew I had to formulate a strategy to make it happen. I decided I would make plans in advance with Jane so I didn't have to worry about Seth's threat to intervene. The next time he asked if I plan to see Jane, I wanted to be able to answer in the affirmative. I went over my conversations with the stranger, trying to find a connection between him and Jane. Nothing came to mind, they were the complete opposites which may have been the connection.

I started a load of laundry and the fifty dollar bill that Seth traded for a beer fell out of my jeans. I studied the bill to see if there was anything unusual about it. It was a crisp, mint-issued piece of paper—nothing out of the ordinary. I decided to put the small windfall to good use.

"Oh, you've got to be shitting me!" Jane found me sitting in her office.

"Nice to see you too, Jane." I smiled feeling terribly foolish.

"Please tell me you are okay. Please tell me that you weren't supposed to be on top of the pyramid last night."

"I'm fine. On top of what pyramid?"

"The cheerleaders had a mishap at practice last night. Someone's shoulder gave way and their whole pyramid came tumbling down. Four of the ten girls suffered sprains or breaks."

I was relieved to know that it was a common accident and nothing that could have involved the man in black.

"I'm not the cheerleader type."

"True. You aren't annoyingly perky enough. Although I believe I have now seen you every day for exactly a week. You might just be annoyingly *something*."

"Am I getting on your nerves?" I bit my fingernail.

"I enjoy your company. I don't know what brought us together but I am very glad we met."

What brought us together. I don't know what brought us together.

"I believe it was a nosebleed that got me in here last week."

"And I see it still hasn't stopped bleeding." She pointed to my face. "Is that why you're here today?"

"No." I reached into my pocket. "I found some cash in my laundry and figured I would pay you for this month's cell phone bill."

"Gray, I told you not to worry about it. Take your extra cash and buy some handkerchiefs."

"I would feel better if you let me pay you. I don't even know if it's enough." I handed her the bill.

"This is more than enough. Let's call it even for two months. Sound fair?"

"Thank you, yes. I have to work at Maple tonight but I was going to go see Katie at Mill Street tomorrow night to get my uniform. I wanted to see if you and Melanie would like to go with me tomorrow night."

"Sure. Actually, we'll see you tonight too. We do go for martinis somewhere every Tuesday. It wasn't just a ploy to see you last week."

"Well, I am glad we've met too." I hoped that was a true statement. "I'll see you later tonight then. And tomorrow? Are you positive you can go to Mill Street tomorrow?"

"Positive." She looked bewildered by my insistence. "We will even pick you up at seven."

"Okay. Thanks." I breathed a sigh of relief.

"Grayson, I'd feel better if you let me check your blood pressure. Your nose bleeds an awful lot. Maybe run a few more tests."

"I'm fine." I blushed. "I'd take a hug though." I couldn't believe I asked that in her office.

She leaned in and gave me a long bear hug. I felt totally safe in her arms and didn't want to let go. I had forgotten how nice it was to feel affection. I wondered if the security I felt was because I longed for touch or if it was because they were Jane's arms that held me. There was no doubt in my mind that if Jane and Seth were some way connected, it was Jane's side I would take if it became necessary to choose.

I was relieved when I got to work and found that the bar was hopping. It was packed, as if everyone who was planning to come on Monday decided to join the Tuesday crowd. Paul was thrilled to see me and the minute I walked in he took my purse and shoved me behind the bar.

"What on earth?" I asked, knowing that Seth was making up for Monday.

"I have no idea but this is the busiest weeknight we've had in years. Keep filling pitchers whether you have an order or not. Use the ice bags if they sit for more than five minutes, it's the only way we will be able to keep up with the Sigmas who have taken over the patio."

I did as I was told and filled every available pitcher with Shiner, Miller and Bud. As the waitresses brought back empty pitchers, I passed them off to Paul to wash and had them refilled within minutes. The frozen margarita machine was empty by five, so we had to resort to making them in the blender. I did my best to keep up one-handed and was relieved to see that Bobby with the broken ribs was called in to run the register. All the available waitresses were called in and Paul's drunken brother volunteered to work the door. People were lined up outside waiting to get in and Paul wanted to make sure each one was of legal drinking age.

Some of the regulars were annoyed by all the students so they surrendered their stools at the bar. Around seven, when I saw two together, I put reserved signs on the seats to hold them for Jane and Melanie. They walked in a few minutes later and tipped me for my thoughtfulness.

"Are you guys having some sort of sale on drinks?"

"No. In fact we got busier after happy hour ended." I wiped the spilled beer on the bar in front of them. "Is there something going on at the stadium tonight?"

"I don't think so. Let me grab the paper." Melanie went outside to the newsstand.

"How's the wrist holding up?"

"Stop worrying about me, Jane. I'm fine."

"Did you eat today?" She laughed.

I realized that in the last thirty-six hours, the only thing I'd eaten was ice cream. "Argh. You're becoming the annoying one."

I threw a beer nut at her and started making their martinis.

"Gray! More pitchers! Just make them all Bud. The Sigmas are too drunk to care." Paul was beaming from the excitement.

"I'll be right back," I said to Jane.

Melanie returned with a newspaper. She spread it out on the bar and the two of them pored over the pages looking for a Tuesday night campus event.

"Anything?" I passed by with three pitchers in my good hand.

"Not yet." Jane was reading an article.

When I made a trip to the storage room to get some replacement liquor bottles, I saw Seth sitting in the corner reading the paper.

"Are you happy? I saw Jane twice today." I balanced on a ladder to reach the higher up bottles.

"Just be careful." His face stayed hidden behind the paper.

"Careful with Jane?"

"No, careful on that ladder. You didn't open it all the way." His voice sounded strained and I fell to the ground.

"Are you okay?" He laughed.

"Was this your doing?" I sat clutching the fingers of my plastered left hand.

"Nope. This one was your fault."

Paul came into the room. "Gray, what's taking so long?"

I glanced up to see Seth walking out the side door. "Little ladder mishap." I climbed to my feet.

"Are you okay? Do you need a break?"

"I already have one, thanks." I held up my wrist and laughed. "I'm fine. You get the bottles and I'll get back to filling pitchers."

The bar was starting to slow down a bit. My head swam when I saw all the cash stuffed in the tip jar. Jane and Melanie were still reading some article in the paper.

Jane glanced up. "Grayson, your nose is bleeding."

"She fell off the ladder," Paul said from behind me. "She's fine. There's no stopping the woman with the gray eyes." He laughed. "Wipe your face, Gray. It's bad for business, they'll think I beat my employees."

I took a napkin to my face and loaded a tray with mixed drinks. A waitress took the tray and handed me another order for the same table.

"Jeez. Haven't these people ever heard of moderation?" I asked. *Moderation.* It occurred to me that the overindulgence I was enabling might have something to do with my previous night's conversation. "Paul, maybe we should start cutting off some of these kids. This is the fifth tray of shots and mixed drinks for those girls in the corner."

"Well, most of the students can walk home from here." He was annoyed by my request.

"Still, we don't want any fights in here and we don't want those women to get attacked in the parking lot by the drunken frat boys." I tried to appeal to his fear of lawsuits.

"Okay. Tell the waitress to start dropping checks to anyone who has had more than four drinks. We are on our last two kegs anyway. What time is it?"

"It's eight twenty-five."

"Holy shit. I'd better call the beer man. Get your friends another martini." He motioned toward Jane and Melanie.

"So did you find anything in the paper that might explain this drunken orgy in here?"

"Nothing. There is a concert on Thursday so you might be busy again then."

"What's so interesting?" I glanced at the front page headline.

"There's an article about that homeless guy who was killed by the train."

"Scott, right?" I set down their martinis.

"Right. He was a bit of a hero. A few years ago in Alabama he pulled a woman and her three kids from floodwaters. A few months after that, he was in Oklahoma and resuscitated a man who had a heart attack on an elevator."

"You're kidding me." I thought about the out-of-state plates on the cars driven by the funeral goers. I remembered Alabama and Oklahoma.

"And on top of all that, he was an organ donor. It sounds gory but what they were able to salvage of his body was sent to three different hospitals around the country, so essentially he saved three more lives."

"And we just knew him as the homeless guy." I felt a little guilty.

"What an interesting twist of fate—his life. Saves all those others and no one is there to save him." Melanie sipped her drink. "Ironic."

Twist of fate. Things were slowly starting to make sense to me—the connection between Seth and Jane and now Scott. I didn't want to put it all together and I prayed I was wrong. I decided that I wouldn't ask Seth about any of it, I would let him tell me what awful thing he was planning. I would do everything in my power to stop it.

The bar eventually slowed down after we started urging people to leave. I was tickled to have made more than three hundred in tips. Melanie and Jane took off after their second martini. Jane figured she would have a busy morning of hung over students hitting the clinic to get excused from class. We reconfirmed our plans to go see Katie at Mill Street and I finally made it home after midnight, exhausted.

Chapter 16

My house was all lit up when I arrived home. Before I left for work earlier I decided to turn on all the lights so that I could tell from a block away if he was there when I returned. I wanted to have that extra distance to prepare myself for being hospitable. I took a hot shower to wash the bar funk out of my hair and forced down a frozen dinner. By one o'clock there was still no sign of the visitor. I crawled into bed and read for a while. I should say that I tried to read but I only stared at the pages and thought about the article in the paper. I told myself that I was reading too deeply into these apparent coincidences and that there was no way everything was related. I repeated this in my head so many times that I was practically singing it as I drifted off to sleep.

"Graaaysooon. Graaaysooon." The voice crooned my name. I rolled over and tried to go back to sleep.

"Grayson, I know you can hear me. Wake up!" He clapped his hands.

I sat up and rubbed my eyes. "What time is it?"

"It is exactly three twenty-two in the morning." He sat on the corner of my dresser.

"Am I dreaming?"

"Nope. You are really seeing me."

"Okay." I sat up. "So, what do you want to talk about?"

"Aren't you forgetting something?"

"Oh, yeah. Sir, may I offer you a beverage?"

"Am I welcome in your home tonight?"

"You are welcome tonight." I yawned.

"I'm fine, stay put." He offered me a cigarette. "Busy night at the bar, eh?"

"Insanely busy. I think I missed your point though." I reached for his lighter.

"A community without moderation." He talked slowly. "I guess it was your point I was trying to prove, but you put a stop to it before it got out of hand."

"Maybe I'm on to you." I chuckled.

"Oh, no need to laugh. I have a feeling you are definitely on to me."

"I have no idea how to reply to that."

"Then don't." He lowered himself to a chair. "So, Grayson Thomas, how do you feel about death."

"I'm opposed to it on forty different levels." I tried to sound glib.

"We are going to discuss it whether you like it or not."

"I guess death is a necessary part of life. The minute you are born you are on the road to dying."

"Why do you think that death is necessary?"

"Well, lots of reasons. Obviously we all can't live forever. I've seen the condition of people who are in their nineties. They look old, they are tired and have a long list of ailments. If we lived forever we would have a world full of wrinkled, bitter, ill people."

"What else?"

"Overpopulation. If nobody died, there would be no room for people to be born. Every inch of land would be wall-to-wall people."

"So you accept the fact that death is inevitable?"

"I accept it. I don't like it terribly but death is a part of life."

"What don't you like about it? If it allows room for babies to be born and it prevents people from getting old and ill, then why don't you view death as a good thing?"

"Because of the sadness that goes along with it."

"Will you be sad about your own death?"

"I will be sad about the death of my loved ones. I could hardly mourn my own death because I don't know when it's going to happen."

"Would you want to know?" He turned his head toward me.

"No. I would rather have it be a surprise. We are all set to die, I'd rather not dread it every day of my life."

"Do you believe that the date and manner of everyone's death is predetermined?"

"Destiny? Fate?" I asked.

"Right."

"I have no idea. There is no way of knowing that."

"What if I told you that it is true that the minute you are born the date of your death is already set in stone."

"Just because you say it doesn't mean it's true."

"Okay, for sake of discussion, let's say that it is true. Let's say that everyone has a ticking clock on the bottom of their foot, some alarms will go off sooner than others. But the bottom line is that the alarms are set and cannot be changed."

"Then I guess it doesn't matter how you live your life. You could chain-smoke and drink a gallon of vodka every day and you won't die until your clock says it's time."

"Very true. Do you think it's possible to change destiny?"

"I would have no way of knowing. Why don't you tell me, for sake of discussion."

"Let's say that you cannot change your own fate but someone else can change it for you. Let's use Hitler as an example."

"Oh, please let's not," I said, cringing.

"Seriously. Let's say that every one of those people in a certain concentration camp was destined to die on a certain day and it was Hitler's orders that made it happen."

"I am not enjoying your example."

"Bear with me. Now let's say that he simply decided not to give the order. Then he would have changed the destiny of all those people."

"But if it was their day to die, if the alarm clocks were set to go off on that day, then something else would have happened to make it right. There might have been a fire or an earthquake."

"Correct. You are understanding."

"So all those people would have died anyway?"

"Unless . . . there is always an addendum to the rule." He leaned in. "Unless someone stepped in and killed Hitler. If someone changed Hitler's destiny on that day, then the lives that were supposed to be taken on that day by Hitler would be saved. Does that make sense?"

"I'm thinking." I tried to get my mind around the concept. "So the only way to change the fate of others is for a third party to change the fate of one individual who is linked to the fate of the parties of the first part?"

"You are making it sound like a legal document. But I do think you are grasping what I am trying to tell you. There are always two parties involved in death, the one who dies and the one responsible for them. If a man is killed in a car wreck, he is person A. The driver of the other car who ran the red light is person B. The only way to save the life of A is for a third party, person C, to intervene and change the destiny of B.

Person C must cause the death of person B, thus changing the predetermined scheme of things for person A. The only way to change someone's fate is to change the fate of the second party, the one responsible for the death."

"Why must any fate be altered then? Why can't the guy simply die in the car crash, then everything is just as it should be."

"You are asking the right questions, Gray."

"But is there always a person B? Surely no one is responsible for the death of a man who choked on a pretzel."

"What about the pretzel maker?"

"A woman who died of lung cancer?"

"What about the tobacco grower."

"A child who fell down the stairs?"

"The babysitter who was supposed to be watching the child."

"Suicide. A teenager who took his own life."

"The pretty girl who broke his heart."

"So no one is responsible for their own death?"

"It's their destiny. The other thing you must see is that everyone is connected. It's like the community you were talking about last night. Everyone is equal, everyone is responsible and the one thing everyone has in common is that everyone must die at some time."

"So every human is a part of one big community where the members are obligated to kill off the other members of the community." I was beginning to see.

"That's the way it works." He sighed.

"So if someone were to ask why do we exist, the answer would be that we exist in order to make the fate of others complete?"

"Don't you think it's possible?"

"It's a lot to absorb but it definitely makes me think." I propped my cast on a pillow. "What does all this have to do with me?"

"That is a conversation for a different night."

"Let me ask you one more thing." I sat up.

"If our death is predetermined the moment we are born, then is it also predetermined whose death we will be responsible for?"

"Yes."

"Can that be changed?"

"Only if someone else changes it for you. Only if a third party causes your death."

"But that doesn't make sense. Is it the third party's destiny to cause the death of that person?"

"Yes."

"But then wouldn't it be that person's fate to die on that day?"

"You are asking the right questions."

"Then tell me the answers."

"I will try to make it simple. The only way anyone can alter the day a person is supposed to die is to cause the death of that person. Murder. Let's say someone named Joe is supposed to be responsible for say, Jill's death and that death is to take place on March third in two thousand ten and he is supposed to hit her in the head with a golf ball. Now Jill is supposed to be responsible for the death of Fred in two thousand seven by running him over with her lawn mower. The only way to save Fred's life is for Joe to murder Jill."

"No one else can murder Jill?"

"No. The person destined to be responsible for your death is the only one who can end your life."

"And it has to be murder?"

"That is the only way to change fate. Joe can't accidently run over Jill on the day of Fred's death. Destiny wouldn't have him in the right place at the right time."

"So he'd have to murder Jill on the exact day of Fred's death in order to save Fred?"

"That's right."

"Who thought up these rules?"

"I couldn't tell you. But they've been this way forever, and they will never change."

"What if someone tried to change the rules?"

"It's not in the cards." He stood. "The sun is coming up and I will soon turn into a pumpkin."

"This was educational. Thanks for filling me in on how the universe works."

"You're welcome." He headed toward the door. "You will see Jane today?"

"She's picking me up at seven." I smiled.

"Things are as they should be. Goodnight, Grayson."

"Aren't you going to wish me a sleep without dreams?"

"Sleep? The sun's coming up. Who has time to sleep?" He tipped his hat and left.

Chapter 17

I tried hard to fall back to sleep. My mind raced from our conversation. I wasn't sure what role I played in this and I still didn't understand the relationship of Seth to Jane to Scott to me but my wheels were turning. My first assumption was that he was trying to get me to kill Jane because she was saving lives, she was holding off death. It would have made sense if a week earlier he played a role in getting Scott killed because he too was saving lives.

Now if Seth worked for the Grim Reaper, then likely he would want Jane and Scott out of the way because they were slowing down the death quota. But based on what I had just been told, the only way to change destiny was to murder someone on the exact day that someone else was supposed to die. Ergo, a doctor or good Samaritan saving lives would not affect the flow of things. I think I had a grasp on the rules—I laid out every angle of the situation but I still couldn't find my place in it.

I still wondered if Seth was real. Suddenly I had a concern that I imagined him and I was hearing voices that were clearly telling me to kill someone. I thought about the things he had said and done over the last week to know if there was anything he did that was not humanly possible. I don't blame him for the bloody noses, unless someone can scare you so badly that your nose bleeds. I tripped over a cat—if he had a role in that I would be surprised. What about the bomb at the school? Seth may not have even been involved. Anyway, any human can plant a bomb. My broken cast? I took two pain pills—he could have broken it while I slept.

I could not think of a single thing that Seth had done that anyone couldn't do. And because no one else saw him doesn't mean he wasn't there. Private investigators hide all the time. Maybe the man has amazing hearing and amazing timing. But what about the dreams? How on earth could my brain come up with those things? Was I predicting the future in my dreams? Maybe it was as Melanie said—dreams are a replay of something you see in the day. Maybe Seth just put ideas in my head. Maybe he sort of hypnotized me—by saying I will have a dreamless sleep, maybe subconsciously I fell for it.

There were too many maybes and nothing else. I decided to give up trying to change the universe. The clock read noon and sleep still wasn't going to happen. I decided to give up on that too and start my day. I was extremely dizzy when I tried to get out of bed. I sat back down and put my head between my knees. The dizziness went away but a pool of blood formed on the floor below me. I tipped my head back and tried to stand. A sharp pain shot through my head and I collapsed. I slowly tried to stand again and was successful. I made my way to the kitchen and got a towel for my nose. I thought about calling Jane but I couldn't stand bothering her again.

The nosebleed slowed to a trickle and the pain in my head went away. I realized that maybe my body was telling me that Seth was still present.

"Hello!" I walked down the hall. "If you're here, speak up." Silence. "Okay, that's it, I'm gonna call the police and tell them that you have broken into my home!" I figured that might be enough to make him speak. "I will never welcome you into my home again!" Still nothing. "I will tell Jane that you want me to kill her!" No response. I knew that if he was present, he would have said something after that last one. I chalked the nosebleed up to lack of food and lack of sleep.

I tried to entertain myself with television and books but I couldn't concentrate. I wished that I hadn't taken the time off from school because at least there, the time wouldn't seem to pass so slowly. I considered going for a drive but I was lightheaded enough to realize that operating machinery wasn't a good idea. I heard the sound of a lawnmower across the street and looked out the window. I saw Minister Ricky tending to the church grounds. I rifled through the refrigerator and managed to come up with two cans of diet soda. I figured it wouldn't be a good idea to offer a beer to a man of the cloth at four in the afternoon.

I walked onto the front porch and waited for Ricky to look up. When he finally did, I waved and smiled. He cut the mower's engine and waved back. I held up the cans of soda and he nodded. I admired his gait as he walked across the street.

"Good afternoon . . . oh, rats." He blushed.

"Grayson."

"I'm so sorry, I should have known from the color of your eyes. Good afternoon Grayson."

"Do you drink diet?" I held out a can.

"I do. I've got to stay in shape to fit under that robe, you know."

"So, you even get to mow the lawn?"

"Yes, I have to do everything around there." He laughed. "But,

I prefer to mow it myself. I enjoy making the church a beautiful home for our families."

"Well, it is a beautiful church. I enjoy living across from such a majestic building."

"Thank you. You should come in sometime. It's even better on the inside, still has all the original fixtures from when it was built in nineteen fifty-four."

"That's wonderful, I will visit one day."

"Are you okay, Grayson?"

"I'm fine. Wow, you are just like your cousin—overly concerned about people."

"My cousin?"

"Yes, I've known Melanie for years. She is a very cool lady."

Ricky laughed. "Yes, she is. Have you met her partner, Jane?"

"Yeah, another cool lady."

"She saved the life of a little boy from our Sunday school class a few days ago."

"I was there. He choked on a toy soldier."

"That's right. Thank the Lord for Jane, that child is destined for greatness."

"Destined for greatness?" It occurred to me that maybe Ricky was the one I should be talking to, maybe he would have the answers I needed to help me fit together the puzzle pieces. "You mean you believe that because he was saved great things will happen to him?" I sounded excited.

Ricky laughed and touched my arm. "Well, maybe so. I meant that any boy who thinks he can eat toy soldiers can do just about anything."

"Oh." I looked down.

"You were expecting something a little more spiritual maybe?" He lowered his eyes to meet mine.

"No, just wondered what you meant."

"Grayson. I asked if you are okay because I noticed you haven't gone to class all week and you have a bit of dried blood on your face."

"I'm taking the week off. I had some dizzy spells and nosebleeds recently, so I was excused from classes to rest."

"You don't look very well rested." He looked apologetic.

"I've had a lot on my mind. You know, like most women in their twenties, I am trying to figure out the meaning of life, the grand scheme of things and how I fit into all of it."

"Oh, that's a plateful. Have you come to any conclusions?"

"Yes. I can't change the world. Things happen for a reason. The world is as it should be." I rolled my eyes.

"Well, those are all truthful statements." He looked at his watch.

"Do you need to be somewhere?"

"I am counseling a newlywed couple at five. I should put the mower away and get changed."

"I hope it wasn't something I said." I made reference to our previous conversation.

He remembered and laughed. "No. You didn't run me off. I could talk to you for hours and maybe one day I will." He stood. "Thanks for the soda."

"Have a good evening, Ricky."

"You too." He smiled. "And Grayson, take things one at a time. God doesn't give you more than you can handle. I know you hear that all the time but it is true. You don't have to solve all the problems of the world, just do what is in your own power and find peace in that."

"Thank you." I stood next to him and was surprised when he gave me a kiss on the cheek.

"Mmm. Now thank you." He smiled, winked and hopped of the porch.

My phone rang at a quarter to seven and I was terrified that it was Jane calling to cancel. I didn't know what would happen if I didn't see her as promised. I was shocked to hear Seth's voice come through the phone.

"Are you still going to see Jane today?" He didn't even say hello.

"She should be here shortly."

"Did you have a nice talk with the Methodist?"

"Just small talk, nothing too deep. I save my in-depth conversations for you." I laughed.

"There's nothing wrong with getting input about our topics as long as you don't say too much."

"Really? I could talk about death tonight?"

"Nothing can change the rules at this point. Don't make them think you're crazy by telling them about me."

"I will be good. Can I ask you something?"

He was quiet for a minute. "Sure. Why not?"

"How did you make it so no one went into the bar on Monday?"

"I put flyers up on campus that it was closed in preparation for Tuesday's big event. I even put one on the front of the bar after you went to work."

"Oh, pretty clever. So what was supposed to be the big event that got everyone into the bar on Tuesday?"

"You'll like this. I didn't put it in writing so Paul wouldn't get sued for false advertising. But I started a very hush-hush rumor that they would be filming one of those 'Girls Gone Wild' films at your bar. I said that only the drunkest of the drunk would get filmed."

"If it was hush-hush then why was there such a great turnout?"

"Do you know any sorority girls who can keep a secret?"

"Man, that's hysterical. You are a smart one, I'll give you that." I heard a car honking outside. "Jane's here, I'll see you tonight?"

"I'll be the one in black." I thought I heard him giggle. "Have fun, you deserve some fun."

I felt so much better about everything after talking to him for those few minutes. It was such a relief to know that he had a humorous side, as well as to know that his manipulations were merely harmless pranks played on college kids. I was excited about a night on the town and even more excited to spark an interesting conversation with my new friends.

Jane was revving the engine of a Sixties Mustang convertible while Melanie laughed hysterically. I couldn't help but melt when I saw what a great, happy couple they made. All I could think of was that it's such a shame I'll have to kill her. Then I laughed hysterically myself because the thought of it was so absurd that I knew it wasn't real. It was at that exact moment that I knew in my soul that it was not Jane I was supposed to kill. I don't know what gave me that feeling but I knew it was a fact.

Ricky stood in front of the church and waved. Melanie and Jane were so preoccupied with the car that they didn't even notice. I waved back and hopped into the backseat. Jane hit the gas and we squealed away like a bunch of teenagers on their way to the mall. They had some punk music blaring from the speakers and were dressed in clothes you would never expect to see on two seemingly conservative women.

"Why are you two so happy this evening?" I shouted over the radio.

"It's the car." Melanie held up her arms like a game show hostess. "I picked it up this morning."

"It's awesome. What is it? A Sixty-seven? A two eighty-nine?"

"Yup. You're good! It was my car in high school. I finally had it completely restored. It was such a piece of shit and they made it look like new." She beamed.

"Well, it's a beauty."

"What do you drive now, Gray?"

"I have a Jeep Wrangler, soft top."

"Makes sense. You've always been the Jeep kind of girl. Jane drives a BMW. I keep telling her that she does not have a BMW personality but she won't trade it in."

"Well, what kind of personality do I have?" Jane sped around a corner.

"Baby, I see you in a Hummer," Mel answered.

"If you see me in a Hummer, you will later see me in a poor house."

"How 'bout a Porsche Boxster?"

"Too small. I like a lot of room for when my brother visits."

"Well, what do you think you are, Jane?" I asked.

"I think I'm a Volvo. I'm all about safety, family and reliability." She was serious and very accurate.

We pulled into the parking lot on Mill Street and carefully put the top up on the classic beauty. I watched the rapport between Jane and Mel again and was almost jealous. I hoped that when I was older I would find someone who brought me as much happiness as they brought each other. They were a bit of an unlikely pair appearance-wise. Jane was short, blond, conservative, with little round glasses that hid huge blue eyes. Then there was Melanie—very tall, dark, long-legged and practically muscular. They looked like polar opposites but somehow it all worked. I listened to them laugh and again I thought it's such a shame I'll have to kill her. My thought didn't seem so funny that time and I felt incredibly guilty about even thinking it. I still knew deeply that it wasn't a true statement but I was repulsed by the fact that it was persistent. I needed a drink.

Katie greeted me at the front door and asked me to join her in the office. The other two went on to find a table on the patio.

"We didn't get to talk much. I got a little heat from the other girls about hiring someone new without an interview or application. I know you have great references but let's chat a bit so I can get the waitresses off my back."

"They want to know my details, huh?"

"You figured me out already." She clapped her hands. "They think you're hot."

"I have no idea how to respond to that, so I won't." I blushed. "Do you need my phone number or address?"

"I got most of that from Melanie after you left on Saturday." She sat on her desk. "I have two questions."

"Shoot."

"Would you be willing to submit to a drug test?"

"Sure, anytime." I didn't bat an eye.

"Just the fact that you're willing is good enough for me. I've met you twice now and both times your nose has been bleeding."

"I'm under Jane's care for that. She ran some tests and all. It's probably allergies or stress."

"Okay. No worries. Second question. Are you comfortable around lesbians? You'll see a lot of PDA in this bar. I want to make sure you won't stare or make anyone feel out of place. I hate to ask but it's important that people feel at home and safe in this bar. I want to make sure you make everyone feel welcome."

"I have no problem with that. I can make anyone feel welcome, trust me." I laughed. "I support anything that makes people happy. I was just admiring what a great couple Dr. Andrews and Miss Winters make."

"Oh, they are a perfect match. They met right after Jane went into remission. She had sold the bar which was really her only source of socialization. When Melanie came along, Jane found such a zest for life again."

I didn't know which statement floored me more. "Jane owned this bar?"

"Yeah. Well, she did. I thought you knew that. Hell, it's called Jane's Mill Street. Pay attention." She rapped me on the head.

"Jane had cancer?" How could I have missed that. "I've only known her a week, you'll have to forgive me."

"Oh. Well, she had a rough battle with breast cancer. I'm just so happy to see her healthy now. I pray that she and Melanie will have a lifetime of happiness together."

"It's a shame I'll have to—" I stopped when I realized I was saying it out loud.

"What's that?"

"Oh, I started to make a bad joke and decided against it." I smiled.

She shot me a funny look. "Okay. Well, have fun tonight. I'll leave your shirts with the bouncer—grab them on your way out and I will see you Saturday at eleven. Do you know how to make a Long Island Iced Tea?"

"I think I can manage." I made a mental note to buy a barkeeper's book and study it.

"Okay." She shook my hand. "Employees drink free. Can I get you a cocktail."

I answered before I knew what I was saying. "Does that mean I am welcome in your home?"

She laughed like I was making a joke. "You are more than welcome."

"Then I'll have a beer in a glass." I clapped my hands feigning excitement. She appreciated the gesture.

I found my friends huddled together at a picnic table with a few other women. I realized that it probably wouldn't be appropriate for me to bring up any of my Seth discussions in front of people I hardly knew. I definitely knew I wouldn't bring up destiny, fate or death now that I knew about Jane having cancer. They made room for me on the bench and introduced me as the wild woman of Melanie's college years. I sat and politely listened to their conversations. Apparently the other women also worked at the university. Two were teachers and one was in administration. It was weird to see faculty out living it up. I always assumed university employees were in bed every night by nine plotting how they would torture students the next day. I zoned out and entertained myself with my own thoughts until Jane caught my attention.

"Gray?" She snapped her fingers. "Are you with us?"

"What? I'm sorry, I was just watching the stars. I didn't mean to be rude."

"I was asking you about that pipe bomb. You were supposed to be in that classroom, right?"

"Yeah. My first class of the week is in that room. If I had gone on Monday, I would have been evacuated with the rest of them."

"I'm glad Ted found it in time. Can you imagine?" their friend Shannon said.

"Yeah. That would have been awful." I tried to clear my head and get into the conversation but my mind was cloudy.

"I feel so bad for him, now he's being investigated by the university for indecent behavior with a student."

"What are you talking about?" Jane, Mel and I asked in unison. We all leaned forward, prepared to hear some juicy gossip.

"Ted Marks. You know, your instructor."

"Yes." I sat up straight.

"Okay, well this is all confidential information. I only know because I work in the right office. Promise you won't tell a soul?" Shannon practically whispered.

"I promise." I was giddy from the secrecy.

"Well, he had been having an affair with one of the male students. Ted Marks is married with three kids. Apparently he has a secret of his own, if you know what I mean." She winked. "Anyway, he was sleeping with one of the boys in your class and he broke it off. I'm told they had a big fight here in this bar a few weeks ago."

"Go on." We all leaned in closer as a plane passed overhead.

"Well, the kid refused to accept the breakup. He told Ted

he would regret it, that he would pay for what he did. The kid
built the bomb in his apartment and on Sunday he broke into
Canon Hall and planted it in Ted's desk drawer. I think the kid
had a change of heart when he realized that it could kill people.
He stood up in the middle of class and told Ted to open his
drawer."

I felt sick to my stomach. Could it have been Kevin? My gut
told me it was, but I didn't want to believe that my dear friend,
my sweet protector could do something so vindictive.

"Do you know the kid's name?" Melanie asked, still
intrigued.

"I do, but I shouldn't say." Shannon was proud of her
knowledge.

"His name is Kevin." I put my head down. "His name is
Kevin Hobbs."

The five women stared at me.

"How did you know that?" Shannon shouted then covered
her mouth realizing that she had just confirmed it.

"Oh, my God. Grayson." Mel put her hand on my back.
"Jane, get her a damp cloth, blood is pouring from her nose."

"I am so sorry Grayson. I had no idea that you would have
known the guy. I should have thought about it, you were in that
class." Shannon's voice sounded calm and sincere.

"I have known Kevin for a few years. We used to work
together at the student union. I knew he was gay because I had a
crush on him and he told me why it would never work." I took
the towel from Jane then lifted my head.

"Tilt your head back, Grayson." Jane pushed the towel closer
to my face.

"He called me incessantly Monday morning after the
explosion. He told me that Marks had found the bomb and
evacuated the building. Kevin was crying. He sounded so
worried, I thought he was worried about me. I thought he was
crying because he is a big drama queen. I had no idea that he was

crying tears of fear and remorse." I took a deep breath. "I had no idea he was capable of something so—" I stopped.

I wondered if Seth knew about the bomb and that's why he told me to skip classes all week. I wondered if it was my fate to die in that explosion and he changed it. But if what he said was true, then someone would have been killed to change my fate . . . murdered. I tried to remember what day it was that Scott was killed. Maybe a train didn't hit him by accident. Maybe he was pushed.

"Grayson, we should take you home." Jane started to stand.

"No. I don't want to go home yet. I'd like to have another beer . . . or ten." I was relieved when they all laughed. "Shannon, what's going to happen to Kevin?"

"I don't know. I am sure it won't be pretty. What he did was very serious. His name will probably hit the news by Friday. You may want to keep an eye out for reporters. They will be after anyone who knows Kevin."

Katie came to our table with a beer for me. "Christ, Jane. What did you do? Did ya punch her?"

"This one's a bleeder, Katie. I'm gonna find out what's causing it though." She looked at me. "If it's the last thing I do."

Chapter 18

Melanie begged me to spend the night at their house. Jane was so worried that something was overlooked on my tests at the hospital that I think she was thinking malpractice. I promised I would go back after the weekend to get another checkup. They reluctantly dropped me off and waited for me to enter the pitch dark house. I flashed the porch light when I was safely inside so they would leave. I didn't turn on any other lights and made my way to the kitchen. Seth was seated at the table behind a paper bag.

"I brought Chinese. I notice that you never eat." He shook the bag.

"Thanks, I'm not hungry." I sat.

"I also put some beer in your fridge, I also noticed you never shop."

"Thank you. That was thoughtful." I got up and opened the refrigerator. "Can I offer you one of your own beers?" I was happy to see a twelve-pack of Corona.

"Am I welcome in your home tonight?"

"A true friend never has to ask. You are welcome tonight, and any other time." I had a lump in my throat.

"Thank you. I am glad you consider me a friend now. I would like a beer in a bottle with a lime. There are lime slices in the plastic bag."

"You're here every night and now you're stocking my fridge. You are a friend, practically a roommate, and if you were thirty years younger you could be my boyfriend." I handed him the bottle.

"Set it down, please." He pushed out the chair next to him. "What would you like to talk about tonight, Gray?"

"Aren't you the one who picks the topics?"

"I sense there is something on your mind. And I saw you at the bar. I know something happened."

I took a deep breath and prepared myself for what I feared I was about to hear. "You knew about Kevin. You knew about him and the bomb."

"Yes, I did."

"Is that why you didn't want me to go to classes this week?"

"Yes and no."

"That's a little evasive. Can you elaborate?"

"Ask the right questions."

"How did you know about the bomb?"

"Last Monday when you stayed at Kevin's he came by your house and took your Jeep. I was watching your house from the parking lot. I thought you might come home later, so I was waiting. When he came back, he unloaded some boxes and bags into that little shed in your backyard."

"No way!" I was stunned.

"I'm a nosy kind of guy, so after he left I went to the shed to see what was there. There were clock parts, explosives . . . you know, just your basic bomb making devices. Then when you were at work last Tuesday night, he came by and got the items."

"That's why he didn't come see me at the Grill."

"He was a little preoccupied."

"So you told me not to go to classes because you knew I would be killed in the explosion."

"I had no idea what day he was going to place the explosive."

"So that's why you told me to take the whole week off?"

"Think about it Gray. If I knew that Kevin was to be the one responsible for your death and I knew he was going to do it with a bomb, wouldn't I also know the exact day? The day of your destiny?"

"Then why did you tell me to skip classes all week?"

"For now, let's just say that it is unnecessary for you to attend classes at this time. I promise that all your questions will be answered in forty-eight hours."

"So you knew nothing about the bomb other than what you got from Kevin's actions?"

"I had no idea . . . see the bomb didn't kill anyone. The bomb was not destined to take lives."

"How do you know that?" I got a beer.

"Because it didn't. If Kevin was to be the one responsible for the deaths of all those kids, then it would have happened. He is not their destiny and he is not your destiny either."

"So no one was meant to die in the explosion."

"No one or it would have happened."

"Too bad Kevin can't use that in a court of law." I sighed. "Okay, I understand the part about how we all have an exact day that we will die and that day cannot change unless a third party intervenes."

"Right."

"And we are all destined to be responsible for the death of others, either directly or indirectly. Either you hit a guy with your car or you manufactured the pretzel that lodges in his throat."

"Correct." He adjusted his hat.

"Is everyone responsible for another's death? Is there anyone who doesn't get the assignment?"

"People who die very young usually aren't assigned responsibility."

"What do you mean by *usually?*"

"For the most part, if a person is to die as a child, they aren't likely to be the second party in another's death. They remain innocent. But there are exceptions, as when a mother dies in childbirth. The child's first assignment takes place the instant he is born."

"First assignment? So we cause more than one death in our lifetime?"

"Most people just get one. Some people get more than one. Think about Hitler . . . his number is too high to count."

"How does it work? Say an airline pilot gets drunk and crashes the plane. He kills everyone on board. So all those people were destined to be killed by that guy?"

"Right, he was their destiny."

"So how did all the people who were assigned to him happen to be on the same plane?"

"Fate . . . it was meant to be. The world times and plans these things to get everyone in the right place at the right time. It's like one giant travel agency in the sky."

"But you can't be responsible for your own death. If the pilot died from flying the plane while he was drunk, isn't it his fault?"

"No, it's the fault of the guy who poured him the drink that put him over the edge."

"The bartender?"

"Correct." He held up his beer.

"Then wouldn't the bartender be responsible for killing all the people on the plane?"

"Not technically. There is a thin line on the rules. The responsibility lies with the person who has the most direct route."

"Then wouldn't the woman who sold the pretzels to the choker be a more direct route than the guy who manufactured them?"

"Yes. I was using a general example."

"And if your wife handed you the pretzel that killed you, wouldn't she be the responsible one?"

"Yes. Like I said, I was using an example, but now you understand the technicalities."

I sipped my beer and let it all soak in. I felt better knowing that I wasn't supposed to die in the explosion but I still didn't understand why Seth was telling me all this. I decided that the best thing was to try to grasp the whole concept. Knowing how it all worked might open my eyes to what I was supposed to do.

"Obviously your assignments to cause death are to take place before the day you are set to die. Nobody can cause death after they are dead, correct?"

"Correct. Now you can kill and die on the same day, even at the same exact second. If you shot someone and then shot yourself."

"Wow. How do you know all this?"

"Someone approached me a long time ago much as I am approaching you now."

"Did that person die? Was he assigned to you? Were you assigned to him? Was there a third party?"

"So many good questions. None of which I can answer right now."

"Forty-eight hours, huh?"

"That's right. It will all make sense by then."

"Everyone is connected. What a crazy thought. It's like an extension of that six degrees of separation theory."

"We are all in this together." He retrieved his beer and handed me one.

"A homeless guy was killed recently. He was a hero and saved a lot of lives."

"I read the story." Seth's tone was guarded.

"I don't even want to know if he is connected to you and me. But I am curious about another kind of destiny." The thought just occurred to me.

"You are going to ask if heroism is predetermined."

"That's exactly what I was going to ask." I laughed.

"You do ask the right questions." He held up his beer in a toast.

"Is it already decided whose lives we will save?"

"No. See, you can't save a life if that person was set to die. People die on their scheduled day no matter what."

"But Scott pulled three people from a flood, if it wasn't for him, they would have drowned."

"No, they would have lived. If they were supposed to die, they would have died. What Scott did was save them from harm. We are all assigned to help others. We are all given the job of saving people from serious injury. One of those children might have gone into a coma, the mother might have hit a tree and become paralyzed. He saved them from a life of misery."

"So doctors, like Jane?"

"And your friend Frankie. She has quite a road ahead of her. Doctors are wonderful people. It is predetermined for them to help so many people. It's a shame that when a doctor loses a patient that they don't realize that it was out of their control. They can't save a person's life but they can help that person get back to health."

"So the child who choked on a toy last week . . ."

"She did not save his life. He was not scheduled to die. But what she did do was prevent serious brain damage."

"If he was set to die in twenty years, he could have lived it in a coma. But thanks to Jane he will live the next twenty years as a healthy person?" I was awed by this idea.

"That's right."

"Paralysis, illness, handicaps . . . those are not predetermined?"

"Nope. Shit happens. Injuries and illness keep life interesting. If no one is assigned to pull that toy from your throat, then you will serve your time comatose. They deal out the heroism like a lottery system. Not everyone gets to be saved from injury. No one gets to be saved from death."

"Unless there is a third party intervention, which apparently is damned near impossible."

"You got it, kid!" He slapped his knee.

I recalled previous conversations and tried to think of anything that I could follow up on. I wanted to get everything exactly right.

"A few nights ago . . . I made a remark that you threw back at me." I leaned in.

"You said, 'Nobody chooses death.'"

"That's right."

"So that is a true statement then."

"No one does choose death, Grayson. Death has already been chosen for you."

We talked another half hour about heroism and life in general. Seth finally left around four and I think the old guy was a little tipsy. I would have worried about him, but I knew nothing would happen to him or me for at least forty-eight hours. I did wonder where he went after he left my place. I wondered where he slept or if he slept. I wondered who came into his life all those years ago and told him what he was telling me. I wondered if that person died.

I knew that someone was going to die. It was a surreal feeling. I knew it would be Seth or Jane or even me. I couldn't stand the thought of losing either one of them. In the past week, they had both become the most important people in my life. I was at peace with the idea of my own death. It occurred to me that maybe that was why Seth was present. Maybe he was telling me all this so I could find the peace I needed to let myself go. If it was already set in stone and nothing could change it, then there was nothing I could do but accept it.

A few questions were still unanswered. New ideas popped into my head faster than I could count. I wanted to know if there was such a thing as "natural death." I wanted to know about my dreams, how Seth caused or prevented them. And the most important question of all: What happens to the universe if there is a third party intervention.

Chapter 19

I slept until noon and lay in bed thinking about the universe until one. I kicked myself for wasting what could potentially be one of my last days on earth. I thought about what I needed to do, things I needed to resolve if I was indeed about to die. I felt guilty that I had been spending so much time with my new friends that I hadn't taken time to keep in touch with my family and old friends. I resolved to make it right. I decided to spend the afternoon on the front porch with the telephone and the expensive bottle of wine I was saving for a special occasion. I heard a line in a movie once and it resonated in my head: *Get busy living or get busy dying.* I decided to get busy living, I had been dying my whole life.

The first person I called was Frankie.

"Why aren't you in class, jackass?" She was at a Mommy and

Me swim class.

"I've decided to take the week off."

"Well, can I call you this weekend? I'm in the pool now and am swamped for the next two days."

"I'm not sure I'll be around this weekend." She didn't know how literal I was being. "I just wanted to tell you that I am very proud of you. I think going to medical school is a great idea and there is no doubt in my mind that you will be an amazing doctor."

"Well, I'm not sure it will happen. Hefty Harry is telling me that it's not feasible." I heard the disappointment in her voice.

"I have it on great authority that it will happen. I am very proud of you and I love you very much. You are my best friend, Frankie."

"I love you too. I appreciate the support." She was quiet for a second. "Are you drunk?"

"No." I had to laugh. "Just at peace with the universe."

I called my other two former roommates and told them pretty much the same thing, that I was proud of them, that I was honored to be a part of their life. They both also accused me of being drunk. I told them I was high on life and they told me I was nuts. I called a few of my old boyfriends and forgave them for being lousy . . . just for being lousy. I called Paul at Maple Street Grill and told him that I couldn't come in until further notice. I thanked him for being the best boss in the world.

I called my aunts, uncles, cousins and high school friends. If I had their number, they got a call. If they weren't home, they got messages. I saved my parents for last. My dad was off at some handyman's convention but my mom was free to chat as usual.

"You're not at class?"

"No. I'm off for a while. How's business?"

"It's picking up. If you're off from school, do you want to come home?"

I thought about it for a minute. Maybe going home would

be a good idea. I could be with the ones I loved. If I was set to die, it would happen no matter where I was. Seth might follow me there . . . but what if I needed Jane. I wasn't sure if she was an integral role, so I decided I would stay close to her. Of course, what if it wasn't me who was to die . . . it still wouldn't matter where I was. I was confused but determined to stay put.

"I think I'll stick around here. But I promise, you will be seeing me very soon." She had no idea what a morbid statement that was.

"Well, good. I miss those gray eyes."

"Mom, where did I get my eyes? Did Grandma have gray eyes too?"

"No. Her eyes were blue. You must have gotten them from the mailman. I've never seen eyes like yours in my life and neither has your father. We always thought that you were going to be exceptional because no one in the world had eyes like yours. And we were right. You are an exceptional woman."

"Mom, I've done nothing important with my life. I was an average kid and now I'm an average adult." I had let them and myself down.

"You are hardly average. You have more heart and more soul than anyone on this earth. I believe you will change the world."

You will change the world. What happens to the universe if there is a third party intervention?

"I hope so, Mom. I hope you and Dad know how much I love you. I am proud to be your kid." I tried not to cry.

"We know that. You've always made us feel loved, Gray Gray." She did start to cry. "And you know how much we love you?"

"I feel it every day of my life. I know you love me." I had said exactly what I had called to say. "Okay. I need to run, I have to go prepare to change the world." I laughed, although I was being serious.

"You don't have to do it all at once. One piece at a time, okay?"

I liked her use of the word "piece." It made me think of the puzzle I was trying to complete.

"Okay. I promise. Give Dad a huge hug."

I hung up before she could respond. I tried to let myself cry but the tears wouldn't come. I felt better knowing that I had contacted everyone I cared for. I wondered how many of them had been destined to save me . . . if I had to guess, they had all saved me from harm at one time or another. Even now, realizing how much love I had in my life, the conversations I had just had saved me from guilt and sadness. I wondered if it's possible to save someone from their own emotions. I figured that would be something Melanie might understand. She seemed to be in touch with things like that. I thought about calling her but I saw Ricky standing in front of the church, looking at me.

"Whatcha doin' mister?"

"Watching you." He laughed.

"Why would you want to do that?"

"Because you have been on that swing and on the phone for four hours. I thought maybe it was stuck to your ear."

"Nope." I pointed to my ear. "I removed it before it attached itself permanently."

"Good! I won't have to call Jane to remove it for you."

"Hey, I am about to open a hundred-dollar bottle of wine. It would mean the world to me if you shared it with me."

"Are you asking a man of the cloth to have a drink with you?" He smiled.

I wasn't sure if he was allowed to drink and maybe he thought I was flirting. I was about to backtrack but he spoke first.

"I would love a glass!" He crossed the street.

I opened the bottle and slowly poured it. "I'm sorry, I only have one wine glass. Do you mind sharing? I'd hate to drink this out of a coffee mug."

"I don't mind. You take the first sip."

I took a sip of the beautiful wine. It was the best thing I had tasted in my life and I was delighted to share it with Ricky.

"May I ask you a question?"

"You just did." He laughed and took a sip from the glass. "This is delightful, thank you."

"Do you believe in fate?"

"As in a beautiful woman renting the house across the street from the church of a handsome minister?"

"I . . . um. I . . ."

"Please continue. Do I believe in fate?" He handed the glass back to me.

"When someone dies and people say well, that was God's plan, do you think there is a plan for our deaths?"

"If it is his will. The Divine Plan. I believe that God does have a plan for each of us."

"What if . . . and please tell me if I am asking something inappropriate . . . what if we are all predestined to be the cause of someone else's death? Do you think that is possible."

"I think anything is possible, Grayson. But if we are destined to be the cause of someone else's death it would sure make you think about how you treat other people."

"How do you mean?"

"Well, give me a moment to think of an example."

I could tell that he was a very thoughtful man. One who always tried to say the right thing and I knew I had found the right person to talk to.

"Let's take my cousin Melanie for example."

"Okay."

"As you may know, Melanie is a lesbian." He smiled and winked like it was supposed to be a secret.

"Yes, I am aware of that fact." I winked back.

"Okay. Well, there are terrible people out there who hate people for being gay. They even use religion as an excuse to hate them. Which I personally think is odd because if anything, religion would teach us to love our neighbor. So, say, God forbid it should ever happen to Melanie, but say that an angry, spiteful man verbally attacks Melanie every single time she leaves her house. Say he holds up evil signs and waits for her to walk by so he can call her names. Wouldn't it be ironic if she was the one destined to be the cause of his death?"

"That would be ironic." I laughed at the idea.

"If he had known that she would be the one responsible for his demise, then he might have treated her better. What if she was allowed to choose the manner in which he would die. Well, had he been nicer, she might make it so he went peacefully in his sleep. And I know Melanie has a sweet heart and would never be vengeful. But since he was terrible to her, she might decide that he should have a slow painful death, feeling that it would serve him right. So, if we knew that others made that decision for us, it might behoove us to be kinder to everyone." He took a long sip of wine.

"Wow, that is a wonderful perspective. So, if for no other reason, that's why we should love our neighbor. It's like the Beatles song . . . 'and in the end, the—'"

"Love you make is equal to the love you take."

I looked deep into his eyes and felt complete tranquility. There was nothing else to be said between the two of us. We had figured out the meaning of life right there on my front porch with a bottle of cabernet sauvignon. The meaning of life really was to do unto others, to love and to be loved, to be kind and generous. We are all part of the same community, we are all part of the Plan and we are all equals.

We drank half the bottle of wine. I wanted to save the other half for Seth. Ricky headed back to the church around seven. I watched the sun fall into the horizon. It was so beautiful that I wanted an encore. I hoped I would be up early enough to watch the sun rise again in the morning. I gathered my things and stood to go inside. As I opened the door, a voice came from behind me.

"Ten days in a row."

I turned around to see Jane, Melanie and Fletch standing on the sidewalk.

"What's that?"

"I have now seen you every day for ten days. I think I am getting addicted to your presence." Jane grinned.

"Or maybe I am to yours. Out for a walk? Beautiful night for it."

"Gorgeous evening. We passed by earlier, but you were in deep conversation with my handsome cousin." Melanie made a kissing noise.

"We had a great talk. I wish I had met him years ago when I moved in."

"Oh, he wouldn't have been here then. He only started at this church last Sunday after the previous minister died."

I didn't let my mind jump to conclusions. I let the information fall to the top of the pile of pieces. I made no assumptions because everything was as it should be and I was at peace with that.

"I have a pitcher of tea. Would you like to stay for awhile?"

"Sure." They headed up the steps to the porch. Melanie tied Fletch's leash to the swing.

The house was dark and I didn't bother turning on any lights. Jane and Melanie waited on the porch while I went inside to get the tea. Seth was sitting at the kitchen table with his hat tilted over his face.

"Join us for some tea?"

"I wish I could."

"Will I see you later?"

"We have our last conversation tonight. I will wait for you. Take your time." He handed me a bag. "I brought you a burger."

"Thank you. I will eat it later. I haven't had much of an appetite lately."

"I know. And I'm sorry, I'm sure I haven't helped."

I turned to head back outside, but stopped. "Seth, how come everything seems so final? It's like I'm seeing everything and feeling everything for the first time, but it almost hurts, like inherent sadness."

"Everyone feels that sadness at one time in their life. You don't know what the future holds, so you don't know if this is the beginning or the end."

"But no one knows what the future holds."

"But everyone thinks that today is the first day of the rest of their life. You have a fear that today is the last."

"Either way, everything is beautiful. It's almost like everything has a glow, an aura."

"I know. Enjoy your evening, Grayson. I will be here, waiting."

"Oh, the rest of the bottle is for you." I set the wine on the table. "It's a beauty."

"Thank you."

"Were you talking to someone?" Jane took the pitcher.

"Just the kitties. I had to explain to them why dogs can go outside and cats cannot."

"And why is that?"

"Because of their enemies." I smiled.

"Enemies?"

"Yes, Michelin, Goodyear, Pirelli . . . the bad guys."

"Ah. You seem different today, Grayson. Very somber. Is it because of Kevin?"

"No. I am just enjoying my time off."

"Yeah, weren't you supposed to work tonight?"

"I called in. I wanted to spend the day appreciating."

"Appreciating what?"

"Just appreciating." I sat next to Fletch.

Melanie and Jane weren't very talkative. It felt a bit awkward and I figured they sensed that I was feeling a little lost. There were things I wanted to talk to them about but I wasn't sure how to approach it. After a few minutes of internal debate, I decided to keep things light. I didn't know what my relationship was destined to be with Jane and I didn't want to say anything that might jeopardize Seth's plan.

"So do you guys have big plans for the weekend?"

"Fishing for an invitation again?" Melanie laughed.

"No. I'm going to lay low." I just wasn't sure how low.

"Well, we won't be around anyway."

I felt a wave of panic fall over me. What would happen if Jane wasn't around?

"Where are ya'll going?" I tried to sound casual.

"I'm going to San Antonio for a family reunion." Melanie rolled her eyes. "Jane lucked out and has to work."

I breathed a sigh of relief. "Oh, I'm sure she would have loved to go with you."

"Um, sure. Breaks my heart to miss it." Jane tried to sound serious.

"You work all weekend?"

"Just Saturday night and Sunday afternoon."

I did some math and knew that I was down to my last twenty-eight hours until all my questions were answered. That meant Friday night was alarm clock time and Jane would be close. I knew that everything was in place, the way it was planned, and I was ready to start the countdown.

"I'm suddenly feeling awfully tired." Which was the truth.

"You look exhausted. Are you feeling okay?"

"Tired, otherwise I feel pretty good."

"You go get some sleep. We need to get Melanie and Fletch packed anyway."

I scratched Fletch behind the ears and he pumped his leg. I stood to say good-bye and it occurred to me that this was the first good-bye I made in person, potentially the last good-bye and the last hug forever.

"Melanie, have a safe trip. It was so wonderful to see you again." I started crying.

"Gray, I'll be back on Monday. We'll be at the Grill on Tuesday." She sounded concerned.

"I know," I sniffed. "I don't know what's gotten into me. I guess I'm just tired."

"I'm sure I'll see you tomorrow, Gray. We are on a roll, no reason to stop now." Jane took my hand.

"I know for a fact that I will see you tomorrow. I just don't know when. Can I call you?" I hoped I hadn't said anything that might mess with the plan.

"Call me anytime, day or night." She looked at Melanie. "You know what I mean."

Melanie laughed. "Yes, I know. I'm not worried that you two will run away together."

They stepped off the porch and I wasn't ready yet.

"I need a hug." I stared at Fletch.

They both walked back up the steps and embraced me at the same time. It took all my energy to fight the tears that overcame me. I held them there for a few minutes and finally let them go. I watched my friends as they walked toward home. When they disappeared around the corner, I finally let the tears flow. I felt a hand on my shoulder and turned to find the warmth of Seth's arms. He led me into the house and helped me onto the sofa. He brought me the last glass of wine and turned on some music.

Chapter 20

"You have a million questions, don't you." He stroked my hand.

"You are real. Someone imaginary couldn't hold me so close."

"I am a real live breathing person."

"How did I know that your name was Seth?"

"My name isn't Seth. You called me that and I accepted it to keep the anonymity."

"What is your name?"

"My name is Michael."

"Where did I come up with the name Seth?"

"I don't know. Maybe you thought I was death personified. Seth would be a logical name in that case."

"That's true. Can I still call you Seth?"

"You can call me anything you want."

He sat on the sofa next to me and I leaned my head on his shoulder.

"How did you mess with my dreams?"

"I didn't. I knew you were having nightmares. My wishing you a dreamless sleep was my attempt at using the power of suggestion."

"But I had dreams about you. I dreamed you were on the swing."

"And you saw me on the swing at your grandma's house. It was a memory."

"But I dreamed about the bomb. I heard it in my dream and I heard the sirens."

"No. You were half asleep when the bomb went off, you were still half asleep when the sirens followed. You didn't dream it, you just weren't aware that you were half awake."

"How long have you been following me?"

"Eighteen years."

"Since I was six?"

"Yup. You were adorable at age six."

"Have you been there every day for the last eighteen years?"

"No. I was there when your Grandma died. I was there when you went to your first dance."

I thought for a moment. "That night I saw you by the pool at my parents' house, you were there."

"Yes, if you recall, your first dance was that same weekend."

"When else were you there?" It was like looking through a photo album of my life.

"I was there when bought your first car. I was there again when you wrecked it. I saw you go to the prom, I watched you graduate from high school. I was there when you moved into this house and I was there when you got that tattoo."

"You were in Mexico?" I couldn't believe that he followed me to another country.

"I chose the tattoo for you. I kept moving it to the top of the pile and you finally picked it. It just made sense that you have that torch."

"But doesn't it mean everlasting life . . . immortality?"

"It also means wisdom. And you definitely have the wisdom now." He sighed.

I could hear his heart beating.

"So you have always been there for me?"

"Always." His heart beat faster.

"You are the constant in my life."

"That's a beautiful way to look at it, Grayson. I appreciate that perspective more than you can imagine."

We listened to the radio and sipped our wine. I didn't care what time it was or how much time was left. As long as it was dark, I knew Seth was by my side.

"I asked the Methodist what would happen if people were predestined to be a role in other people's death. Was it okay to ask him that?"

"Sure, that was okay. What did he say?"

"He said it would make you think about how you treat people if you knew there was a chance they got to choose your method of death."

"That's a great answer, He's a good man, I like him."

"I like him too." I pictured Ricky's smile. "So you liked his answer?"

"Yes. There is a word for that, you know."

"No, what's the word?" I couldn't believe the answer was already out there.

"The word is karma."

"That's right! Oh, that's cool. It's karma." I couldn't wait to tell Ricky.

"What else do you want to know?"

"You still aren't going to tell me why you are here? Why we need Jane? If Scott is related to all this?"

"I will tell you tomorrow night. Everything will make sense then." He sighed. "But if it makes you feel any better, Scott is not linked to the three of us in any way. He is just a member of our community who was destined to help people and destined to pass on that day."

"I do feel better knowing that. Thank you."

"What else is behind those beautiful gray eyes?" He stroked my hair.

"Is there such a thing as natural causes? Can't people die of old age?"

"A small percentage of people slip through the cracks. No one is assigned to them and they drift away in their sleep with no responsible party."

"Is there a name for those people?"

"Not technically. Personally, I call them the lucky ones." He laughed.

"I know that a third-party intervention is nearly impossible. It would practically take a miracle, right?"

"Correct."

"But it has happened?"

"It has. Sometimes, but almost never, it happens because of knowledge. One or two of the parties were aware of the rules. Most times that it has happened, it was purely coincidental. A total freak of nature, it goes against all rules and likelihood."

"But you have the knowledge." I shuddered to think what that meant.

"And you have the knowledge now too," he whispered.

"What happens if the rules are broken? What happens if the third party intervenes and saves the first party?"

"The world comes to an end." He tried to sound dramatic.

I hit him in the ribs. "Nuh-huh, you jackass. Seriously, what happens?"

"Destinies are reassigned. The exact second that the wrong person dies on the wrong day, the destiny of the other two is changed."

"Will it make them bad people? They won't be working for the devil or anything like that, will they?"

"No. They will be the same as they always were. They won't even know the reality of what happened."

"So the universe will remain as it should be, Seth?"

"Yes, Grayson. The sun will rise, the birds will sing and all will be as it should be all over again."

Chapter 21

I awoke to the sound of a slamming door, a sound so cold and final that it bolted me from my sleep. The room was still relatively dark and my back was sore from sleeping upright on the sofa. Seth and I had talked almost all night about the scheme of things, my childhood and even about a few aspects of his own life. He showed me a picture of himself when he was my age. He was quite tall and handsome, the type of man I would have liked to know. He told me how beautiful I was when I was twelve, how my hair framed my face and made my eyes look like stone.

He told me how proud he was when I graduated from high school. Never once did I feel uncomfortable with the knowledge of his presence in my life. I felt a certain serenity knowing that he was such a part of me. I grew to think of him as my guardian angel and he was very ill at ease with that analogy. I didn't bother to ask him if he would always be there because I knew that something drastic was about to happen. I knew in my soul, that by the end of Friday, our relationship was going to end. I sat in the darkness petting my cats and wondering who would love them if I was gone.

As the day before, everything I thought about seemed very final. I thought about the last embrace I shared with Mel and Jane. It was so warm and generous. I thought about the kiss that Ricky gave me on my cheek, his light touch held a definite spark. I thought about the comfort of the safety I felt in Seth's arms. I thought about the beauty of the sunset and how I wanted to see the sun rise again. I knew that I only had a few minutes until that opportunity had passed. I wrapped my grandmother's afghan around my shoulders and walked out onto my front porch—the porch that had become such a wonderful extension of my home.

The sidewalk was damp from the spring dew and I enjoyed the delicious feeling of coolness on my bare feet. I sat on my rickety porch swing and let it rock me back and forth while I directed my tired gray eyes to the orange eastern sky. I simply sat and stared and thought how it was the most beautiful thing I had seen in my entire life. I didn't need to see another sunrise, because this one was such a gift, such an amazing testament to the beauty of the universe.

My eyes remained on the sky when Ricky came up the porch steps and sat next to me. I passed him a part of my blanket and held his hand underneath. He never made an attempt to speak, he focused his eyes eastward and squeezed my hand tightly. I leaned into his body and he wrapped his arm around my shoulders. I didn't look his way when tears began rolling from my eyes. I stared at the sky when I felt his gaze move to my eyes. I sat and watched the sky for what seemed like hours while Ricky held me and watched me cry.

When the church bells struck eight, he slowly stood and

stroked my hair. He still never said a word but he kissed me gently on the forehead, which revealed more than any spoken word could. I watched him walk across the damp street and into the beautiful, peaceful building. I took the time to admire the stained glass windows and strong stone structure. Though part of me longed to enter the building, a stronger part of me understood that it was too late.

Although the day was definitely not like any normal day, there were still things I had to do. I had to eat and shower and clean. I paid extra attention to all three of those tasks. I made myself a hearty brunch of pancakes as well as waffles. I took a long, cool bubble bath and talked to the cats as they watched me splash bubbles on the walls. I cleaned the house from top to bottom, did all my laundry and even cleaned out the refrigerator.

I washed my Jeep and left a note inside for anyone who cared explaining there were only three payments left. I set the key on the dash weighing down the last three payment coupons. I finally felt like everything was in order. It was time to see what destiny had in store for me. I walked to the corner market and spent my last ninety-three dollars on two bottles of Moët White Star and two champagne glasses. I knew that this would be the night when others would discover if I was crazy or if the man in black really did exist. I realized that I was to discover the truth as well.

I returned to my beautiful, warm home and lay down on my bed. I did not turn on the television or the radio, mainly because the news of Kevin's confession had hit the media. The only thing I had to keep me company, other than my cats, was the sound of my ticking watch. I lay on my bed and waited, my mind was a complete blank from overuse and exhaustion. I could not formulate a thought and the room around me became a blur. A watery halo enveloped everything around me and I was forced to close my eyes. A trickle of blood fell from my nose and I knew it was time, I knew Seth was present.

"This is it, huh? This is what we've both been waiting for?"

"Yes, Grayson. The time has come."

"Are you going to tell me everything now?"

"Yes, Grayson, the time has come."

He left the room and walked around the house. I heard him unlock the front door and open it. He left the screen door closed. When he returned, he had taken off his coat and hat and brought in the bottles of champagne.

"Are you my destiny, Seth?" My breathing was heavy.

"I am. I am responsible for you, Grayson Thomas."

"How did you know?"

"A man came to me eighteen years ago and told me that I had made a mistake. He told me there was an error in my work. I was not allowed to contact you to make it right. I was assigned to you and there was nothing I could do to change it." His voice was hollow.

"You made a mistake that will lead to my death?"

"Yes. I am so sorry, Grayson." He began to cry.

"What was it?"

"When you were six years old, you were getting headaches. Your parents had some tests run and I was working at the hospital at the time. The doctors ran a CAT scan and I was the one who determined the results. I was in a hurry and overlooked something. You had a cerebral aneurysm."

"But you didn't give me the aneurysm."

"No, but I didn't do my job as savior to warn you about it and as crazy as it seems, I was also assigned to be your destiny because of my mistake. The aneurysm has ruptured and is bleeding into your brain."

"But Jane ran tests, they didn't find it."

"I didn't see it either, it is almost undetectable. I should have looked closer."

"Then Jane should have looked closer too."

"It wouldn't have mattered. Grayson, today is the day you are destined to die." He cradled his head in his arms and cried.

I kept my eyes closed and listened to the sound of his sobbing. I tried to reach out to him but my arms were heavy. I waited for him to recover and asked the only thing that came to my mind.

"Why did you tell me all this? Why did you follow me all those years?"

"I went to find you when you were six to make things right. I tried to tell you of my mistake but that goes against the rules, the words couldn't be spoken. So I followed you and watched you grow up. I hated myself every day because I knew it was my fault that you were to die and I have been dreading this day for almost two decades."

"But it's inevitable. You should have gone on with your life knowing that it's just the way it has to be. Everyone is assigned someone, it's how it all works."

"But I love you. You are like a daughter to me and I cannot allow you to die because of my mistake. Not at your age. You are so young and beautiful and you have such an amazing heart."

"It's okay, Seth. It's fate." I was finally able to stroke his hand.

"I went back to the man who told me about the plan, the assignments. I asked him what could be done to save your life. I begged and pleaded and said I would give my life for yours."

"No, Seth. No." I began to cry.

"He said that I was on the right path. That I must give my life for yours but the only one who can take my life away as a trade for yours is the person who is responsible for me."

"Jane." I whispered.

"Yes." He squeezed my hand. "Jane is my destiny. She is assigned to me."

"How do you know it's Jane, Seth?"

"The man told me."

I repeated the rules. "The only way to save the first party is by the murder of the assigned one. The only one who can murder the second party is the third party who is assigned to him."

"Grayson, you are the first party, I am the second party and Jane is the third. She must intervene and kill me tonight to save your life."

"No. You gave up eighteen years worrying about me. You need to live knowing that I am at peace with my fate. Just let me go, Seth. Please, just let it happen." I was too weak to cry.

My head was pounding, my heart was beating out of my chest. I could no longer open my eyes because of the dizziness and the cloudiness.

"Grayson. Oh, please. This has to happen my way. My day is not so far off. I have led a full life. I have loved and I have felt love. Please, sweet Gray. Please call Jane."

"I can't. I can't let her live with the guilt of having murdered someone. She is a doctor, she could never bring harm to anyone."

"She would kill me if she thought I was hurting you. Call her. Grayson, we are running out of time. Sweet Gray Gray. Take the phone from my hand and call."

"Are you sure, Seth?" My heart was in my throat.

"Yes. I have been planning this moment for so long. I have found a way to change fate but it has to be now. Please, dial the phone."

"But what if I end up in a coma forever?"

"You won't. Your destinies will change the minute I am gone. She will be assigned to save you from harm. She will take care of you and you will be fine."

"What am I supposed to tell her?"

"Tell her I am here. Tell her the door is open and that you are scared." His voice shook. "Gray, I left a butcher knife on the kitchen counter. Tell her that you heard something in the kitchen. She will grab the knife. Then I will yell and you will scream. I will pretend to be hurting you. But I won't hurt you,

Gray. I promise."

"Seth . . ." I cried. "She will call the police. They will get here first."

"No, she is two blocks away. She will run. I've timed it. I timed the cops' response the night you called them about the payphone. Jane will be here first. Call her. Now!"

I couldn't think of anything to say to change his mind. I knew there was no more time to waste. Every time I opened my eyes all I could see were tunnels and hallways. The ceiling was a million miles away. I smelled the faint aroma of vanilla. Every inch of my body was heavy and I knew it was time. I took the phone from Seth and pushed the autodial. Jane answered on the second ring.

"Jane. It's Grayson. He's here. The boogeyman, the man in black. Jane come over. Hurry! I think he's hiding in the kitchen. I'm in my room. Oh, Jane please hurry!" I didn't have to fake the sound of fear. I was terrified.

"I'm on my way, Grayson."

"The front door's open, he got in the front. Hurry!"

"Stay calm. I'm coming, Gray."

I hung up the phone and rested my head on Seth's arm. He stroked my hair.

"This is it then." He smiled.

"Thank you for giving me your life, Seth."

"Thank you for sharing yours, Grayson." He kissed my hand. "You're gonna change the world. You will have an amazing life. I love you."

"I love you too."

I heard Jane enter the house. I heard the squeak of the hardwood floors as she tiptoed down the hall. She did as Seth said she would. She went into the kitchen and found the knife. The minute we heard the sound of the steel sliding off the counter we started our play.

"Jane! Help!" I screamed as loud as I could, again not having to fake the fear.

"Quiet!" Seth pushed his hands onto my shoulders and looked deeply into my eyes as he mouthed the word good-bye. "I told you I'd kill you if you called anyone!"

Jane burst into the room and plunged the butcher knife into Seth's back.

I listened to his breathing as it got slower and slower, then finally stopped. His body went heavy against mine and I closed my eyes. I felt peaceful being so close to him. I felt so calm that I drifted off to sleep.

Epilogue

"I think she's waking up. Frankie, go get her parents." Jane's voice rang in my ears and I was reminded of the church bells.

"Grayson. Are you awake?" Melanie's voice came from the other side.

"Grayson, if you can hear me, squeeze Ricky's hand." Jane whispered. I squeezed my hand as tightly as I could.

"She can hear you." Ricky's voice was jubilant.

I opened my eyes and saw the faces of my true friends.

"Grayson, it's so wonderful to see those gray eyes!" Melanie danced.

"You're going to be just fine." Jane felt my pulse.

I looked around the room hoping to find Seth. Then I remembered he was gone.

"What happened?" My voice squeaked.

"You just had surgery. You had an aneurysm." Jane spoke slowly. "It burst."

It was as Seth said. Everything. Jane did save me.

"Thank heavens you called me." Jane sat on the bed.

"I called you." I meant it as a statement, not a question.

Jane accepted it as a question. "Friday night, right before midnight you called me. You said you were in terrible pain and couldn't move. You said everything was hazy and that your heart was racing."

That's not what I said. Did she forget about the man in black?

"I ran to your house. I found you lying on the floor of your living room." She stroked my hair. "You were holding a bottle of champagne."

"Am I going to live?"

"You are." Ricky whispered in my car and kissed my cheek.

"So everything is as it should be."

"So the universe will remain as it should be, Seth?"

"Yes, Grayson. The sun will rise, the birds will sing and all will be as it should be . . . all over again."

Publications from Spinsters Ink

P.O. Box 242
Midway, Florida 32343
Phone: 800-301-6860
www.spinstersink.com

A POEM FOR WHAT'S HER NAME by Dani O'Connor. Professor Dani O'Connor had pretty much resigned herself to the fact that there was no such thing as a complete woman. Then out of nowhere, along comes a woman who blows Dani's theory right out of the water.   ISBN: 1-883523-78-8 $14.95

WOMEN'S STUDIES by Julia Watts. With humor and heart, Women's Studies follows one school year in the lives of these three young women and shows that in college, one's extracurricular activities are often much more educational that what goes on in the classroom.   ISBN: 1-883523-75-3 $14.95

THE SECRET KEEPING by Francine Saint Marie. The Secret Keeping is a high stakes, girl-gets-girl romance, where the moral of the story is that money can buy you love if it's invested wisely.
                    ISBN: 1-883523-77-X $14.95

DISORDERLY ATTACHMENTS by Jennifer L. Jordan. 5th Kristin Ashe Mystery. Kris investigates whether a mansion someone wants to convert into condos is haunted.   ISBN 1-883523-74-5 $14.95

VERA'S STILL POINT by Ruth Perkinson. Vera is reminded of exactly what it is that she has been missing in life.
                    ISBN 1-883523-73-7 $14.95

OUTRAGEOUS by Sheila Ortiz-Taylor. Arden Benbow, a motor-cycle riding, lesbian Latina poet from LA is hired to teach poetry in a small liberal arts college in northwest Florida.

ISBN 1-883523-72-9　$14.95

UNBREAKABLE by Blayne Cooper. The bonds of love and friend-ship can be as strong as steel. But are they unbreakable?

ISBN 1-883523-76-1　$14.95

ALL BETS OFF by Jaime Clevenger. Bette Lawrence is about to find out how hard life can be for someone of low society standing in the 1900s.

ISBN 1-883523-71-0　$14.95

UNBEARABLE LOSSES by Jennifer L. Jordan, 4th in the Kristin Ashe Mystery series. Two elderly sisters have hired Kris to discover who is pilfering from their award-winning holiday display.

ISBN 1-883523-68-0　$14.95

FRENCH POSTCARDS by Jane Merchant. When Elinor moves to France with her husband and two children, she never expects that her life is about to be changed forever.

ISBN 1-883523-67-2　$14.95

EXISTING SOLUTIONS by Jennifer L. Jordan. 2nd book in the Kristin Ashe Mystery series. When Kris is hired to find an activist's biological father, things get complicated when she finds herself fall-ing for her client.

ISBN 1-883523-69-9　$14.95

A SAFE PLACE TO SLEEP by Jennifer L. Jordan. 1st in the Kris-tin Ashe Mystery series. Kris is approached by well-known lesbian Destiny Greaves with an unusual request. One that will lead Kris to hunt for her own missing childhood pieces.

ISBN 1-883523-70-2　$14.95

Visit

Spinsters Ink

at

SpinstersInk.com

or call our toll-free number

1-800-301-6860